LISA and LOTTIE

ERICH KÄSTNER was born in Dresden, Germany in 1899. He was well known for his poetry and prose, and received wide acclaim for his much-loved book for children, EMIL AND THE DETECTIVES, which has been translated into twenty-six languages.

LISA and LOTTIE
Erich Kästner

Illustrated by Victoria de Larrea

Translated by Cyrus Books

AN AVON CAMELOT BOOK

Originally published in German under the title *Das Doppelte Lottchen* by Atrium Verlag A.G. Zurich

According to the Fry Readability Scale this book has a 6th grade reading level.

AVON BOOKS
A division of
The Hearst Corporation
105 Madison Avenue
New York, New York 10016

Frist Camelot Printing: March 1982

Library of Congress Cataloging in Publication Data

Kästner, Erich, 1899-1974.
  Lisa and Lottie.

  (An Avon Camelot book)
  Translation of: Das doppelte Lottchen.
  Summary: When they meet for the first time at summer
camp, two ten-year-old girls discover they are twins and
agree to exchange identities in an attempt to
reconcilate their divorced parents.
  [1. Family life—Fiction.   2. Twins—Fiction.
3. Divorce—Fiction]   I. De Larrea, Victoria, ill.
II. Title.
PZ7.K118Li 1982   [Fic]   690-11545
                             AACR2

LISA and LOTTIE

*Bohrlaken on Lake Bohren • Girls' camps
like beehives • Twenty new girls • Curls
and braids • On biting off noses • A King of England's
twin • On the difficulty of getting smile-wrinkles*

Do you happen to know Bohrlaken? I mean the village in
the mountains—Bohrlaken on Lake Bohren? Odd—none of the
people I ask seem to know Bohrlaken. Maybe Bohrlaken is one
of those places known only to the people I *don't* ask. Such
things do happen.

Well, if you don't know Bohrlaken on Lake Bohren, then
of course you have never heard of the summer camp of Bohrlaken on Lake Bohren either. But never mind. Girls' camps
are as alike as peas in a pod; if you know one, you know them
all. And if you happen to stroll past one, you may think it is
a giant beehive. Such a hum of shouts, laughs, giggles, and
whispers. These camps are beehives of happiness and high
spirits. And however many there may be, there can never be
enough of them.

Though sometimes of an evening, of course, the gray dwarf
Homesickness sits by the beds in the dormitories, takes from

his pocket his gray notebook and his gray pencil, and with a glum face counts up the tears around him, those shed and those unshed.

But next morning—*presto!*—he's vanished. Then the milk glasses clink and the tongues chatter for all they're worth. Then again swarms of bathing caps race into the cool, bottle-green lake, splash, scream, yelp, crow, swim—or at least pretend to be swimming.

That's how it is at Bohrlaken on Lake Bohren, where the story begins which I am going to tell you. It's a rather complicated story. And now and then you'll have to pay careful attention if you are really going to get the hang of it. It's quite straightforward at the beginning; it doesn't begin to get complicated till later on.

Well, now they are all swimming in the lake, and the most active of all is, as usual, a girl of nine with a head framed in curls and filled with bright ideas, whose name is Lisa. Lisa Palfy. From Vienna.

A gong booms from the house—one, two, three! The children and the counselors who are still swimming clamber up the bank.

"That means all of you," called Miss Ursula, "including Lisa."

"I'm coming!" shouted Lisa. "I'm jet-propelled!"

Miss Ursula drove her cackling flock into the pen—oh, no, —into the house. At twelve sharp they had lunch. And then

they waited, looking forward eagerly to the afternoon.

That afternoon twenty new girls were arriving. Twenty little girls from South Germany. Would they be a lot of old ladies of thirteen or fourteen? Would they bring some decent toys? With good luck one might bring a large rubber ball. Trudie's had no air in it. Brigit had one, but she would not bring it out. She had shut it up in her locker. And locked it.

That afternoon Lisa, Trudie, Brigit, and the others stood around the big, wide-open, iron gates, waiting impatiently for the bus which would bring the new girls from the nearest railway station. If the train came in on time, they ought to be . . .

A car honked. "They're coming!" The bus came speeding up the road, turned cautiously through the gates, and came to a stop. The driver got down and lifted the girls, one after the other, out of the bus. Then he unloaded the trunks, suitcases, dolls, baskets, paper bags, woolly dogs, parcels, umbrellas, thermos bottles, raincoats, knapsacks, blankets, books, specimen cases, and butterfly nets—a gaudy jumble of baggage.

Finally the twentieth little girl appeared at the door of the bus with her belongings. A grave, demure little girl. The driver held out his arms.

The little girl shook her head and, as she did so, her two braids flew out behind her head.

"No, thank you," she said, firmly and politely, and climbed down, calm and sure, from the step. She looked around with a shy smile, and suddenly her eyes opened wide with surprise. She had caught sight of Lisa. Then Lisa's eyes opened wide, too. Startled, she gazed into the new girl's face.

The other girls and Miss Ursula stared from one to the other. The driver pushed back his cap, scratched his head, and forgot to close his mouth.

Lisa and the new girl were the image of each other. One had long curls and the other tight braids—but that was really the only difference between them.

Lisa turned and ran into the garden, as though pursued by lions and tigers.

"Lisa!" cried Miss Ursula. "Lisa!" Then she shrugged her shoulders and turned to shepherd the twenty new girls into the house. And the last to follow, surprised and uncertain, was the girl with the braids.

Mrs. Muther, the camp director, was seated in her office, discussing with the rugged old cook the menu for the next few days.

There was a knock. Miss Ursula came in and announced that the correct number of new girls had arrived safe and sound.

"Very good. Thank you."

"There's something else . . ."

"Yes?" The busy woman looked up quickly.

"It's about Lisa Palfy," began Miss Ursula doubtfully. "She's waiting outside the door . . ."

"Bring the little monkey in." Mrs. Muther could not help smiling. "What mischief has she been up to now?"

"Nothing this time," said Miss Ursula. "It's only . . ."

She opened the door cautiously and said, "Come in, both of you! Don't be afraid!"

The two girls entered the room and stopped—a long way apart from each other.

"Bless my soul!" gasped the cook.

While Mrs. Muther stared speechless at the two children, Miss Ursula went on, "The new girl is called Lottie Horn and comes from Munich."

"Are you related to each other?"

The two girls shook their heads.

"They have never set eyes on each other until today," said Miss Ursula. "Strange, isn't it?"

"Why is it strange?" asked the cook. "How could they have set eyes on each other when one comes from Munich and the other from Vienna?"

Mrs. Muther said in a friendly voice, "Two girls who look so alike are sure to be good friends. Don't stand so far apart. Come, children! Shake hands with each other."

"No!" cried Lisa and folded her arms behind her back.

Mrs. Muther shrugged her shoulders, thought for a moment, and then said, "You can both go."

Lisa ran to the door, yanked it open, and dashed out. Lottie dropped a curtsy and turned sedately to leave the room.

"Just a moment, Lottie," said the director. She opened a big book. "I'll enter your name at once. When and where you were born. And what are your parents' names."

"I've only got my Mommy," said Lottie softly.

Mrs. Muther poised her pen. "First, date of birth?"

Lottie walked down the corridor, went up the stairs, opened a door, and entered the locker room. Her trunk was not yet unpacked. She began putting her dresses, slips, sweaters, and socks into the locker assigned to her. Through the open window came the distant sound of children's laughter.

Lottie held in her hand the photograph of a young woman. She looked at it lovingly and then laid it carefully under her sweaters. When she came to close the locker, her eyes fell on a mirror on the inside of the door. She examined her face gravely and curiously, as though she were seeing it for the first time. Then, with a sudden impulse, she threw back her braids and arranged the hair on top of her head so that it looked more like Lisa Palfy's.

Somewhere a door slammed. Lottie dropped her hands as though she had been caught doing something wrong.

Lisa was sitting on the garden wall with her friends; her brows were puckered in a frown.

"*I* wouldn't stand for it," said Trudie, a schoolmate from Vienna. "The nerve of her—coming here with your face!"

"Well, what can I do?" asked Lisa angrily.

"Scratch it for her," suggested Monica.

"The best thing is to bite her nose off," advised Christine. "Then you've got rid of the cause of the trouble in one stroke!" She swung her legs lightheartedly as she spoke.

"Messing up my vacation like this," muttered Lisa bitterly.

"But she can't help it," remarked chubby-faced Steffie. "If somebody came and looked like *me*, I . . ."

Trudie laughed. "Surely you don't think anybody would be such a dope as to go around looking like you!"

Steffie sulked. The others laughed. Even Lisa smiled a little. Then the gong sounded.

"Feeding time for the wild animals!" cried Christine. And the girls jumped down from the wall.

Mrs. Muther remarked to Miss Ursula in the dining room, "We'll take the bull by the horns and let our little doubles sit together."

The children came streaming noisily into the hall. There was a scraping of chair legs. Waitresses carried steaming tureens to the tables, and filled the plates eagerly held out to them.

Miss Ursula came up behind Lisa and Trudie and tapped Trudie lightly on the shoulder. "You are to sit by Hilda Storm," she said.

Trudie turned and started to say something. "But . . ."

"No objections, please."

Trudie shrugged her shoulders, got up, pouted, and walked away.

Spoons clattered. The chair next to Lisa's was empty. Everyone stared at it.

Then, as though at a word of command, all eyes turned to the door. Lottie had just come in.

"Here you are at last," said Miss Ursula. "Come, I'll show you your place." She led the demure little girl in braids towards the table. Lisa did not look up; she went on furiously spooning her soup into her mouth. Lottie sat down obediently beside Lisa and took up her spoon, though she felt as though her throat were tied up with a piece of string.

The other girls, fascinated, watched the unusual pair from the corners of their eyes. A calf with two—or even three—heads could not have aroused more curiosity. Plump, chubby-faced Steffie was so thrilled that she forgot to shut her mouth.

Lisa could control herself no longer. And, what's more, she didn't want to. With all her strength she kicked out under the table at Lottie's shin.

Lottie winced with pain, and pressed her lips firmly together.

At the grownups' table Miss Gerda, one of the counselors, shook her head and said, "I can't make it out—two absolute strangers and such a remarkable resemblance!"

Miss Ursula said thoughtfully, "Perhaps they're astrological twins."

"What on earth are they," asked Miss Gerda, "astrological twins?"

"I've heard there are people who look absolutely alike without being even distantly related. They just happen to be born in the same fraction of the same second."

"Oh!" murmured Miss Gerda.

Mrs. Muther nodded. "I remember reading of a tailor in London who looked exactly like King Edward VII. You couldn't tell them apart. Especially as the tailor wore the same kind of pointed beard as the King. King Edward summoned him to Buckingham Palace and had a long talk with him."

"And they had actually been born in the same second?"

"Yes. By chance they were able to verify it exactly."

"And what happened after that?" asked Miss Gerda.

"At the King's wish, the tailor shaved off his beard."

While the others were laughing, Mrs. Muther looked thoughtfully across to the table where the two girls were sitting. "We'd better give Lottie Horn the bed next to Lisa Palfy," she said. "They'll have to get used to each other."

It was night. All the children were asleep. Except two.

These two had turned their backs to each other and pretended to be fast asleep. But they were lying with eyes wide open, staring into the moonlit room.

Lisa looked crossly at the queer-shaped silver patch the moon had made on her bed. Suddenly she heard someone

crying quietly, the sobs muffled in a pillow.

Lottie pressed her hands to her mouth. What was it her mother had said when she left . . . *I'm so glad you're going to spend a few weeks with all those happy children. You are too serious for your age, Lottie. Much too serious. I know it's not your fault, but mine. It's because of my work. I'm away from home too much. And when I do get home, I'm tired. And then you haven't been playing like other children, but washing dishes, cooking, and setting the table. See that you come back home with a lot of smile-wrinkles, my little housekeeper!* . . . And now she was lying here in a strange room, next to a bad-tempered girl who hated her because they happened to look alike. She sighed softly. And she was supposed to get smile-wrinkles! Lottie continued to sob softly to herself.

Suddenly her hair was awkwardly stroked by a strange little hand.

Lottie stiffened with fright. Lisa's hand went on shyly stroking her hair.

The moon looked in through the big dormitory window and saw two little girls lying in their beds, side by side, not daring to look at each other. And the one who had just been crying was slowly putting out her hand and feeling for the other's hand as it stroked her hair.

Lisa and Lottie did not dare look at each other next morning when they woke up, or when they ran in their long white nightgowns to the washroom, or when they dressed at neighboring lockers, or when, on neighboring chairs, they drank their breakfast milk; not even when they ran side by side along the lake shore and, later, played singing and dancing games with the counselors and made daisy chains. Only once did their eyes meet in a fleeting glance, and then, frightened, they looked quickly away again.

Now Miss Ursula was sitting in a meadow, reading a wonderful novel which had something about love on every page. Now and then she lowered the book, and her mind went far away as she thought of Mr. Rudolf Rademacher, the engineer who roomed at her aunt's house.

Meanwhile, Lisa was playing ball with her friends. But her thoughts were not on the game. Often she looked around as though searching for someone who was not there.

Trudie asked, "When are you going to bite the new girl's nose off?"

"Don't be such an idiot!" snapped Lisa.

Christine looked at her in surprise. "Well! I thought you were mad at her!"

"I can't bite off everybody's nose when I'm mad at them," retorted Lisa coldly. And she added, "Besides, I'm *not* mad at her."

"But you were yesterday," insisted Steffie.

"And how!" said Monica. "At supper you gave her such a kick under the table that she nearly yelled."

"You see?" said Trudie with evident satisfaction.

Lisa bristled. "If you don't shut up at once," she cried fiercely, *"you'll* get a kick on the shins!" And with that she turned and ran off.

"She doesn't know what she wants," remarked Christine, shrugging her shoulders.

Lottie was sitting alone in the meadow. On top of her head was a little daisy-chain crown, and she was busily making another. Suddenly a shadow fell in front of her. She looked up.

Lisa was there, hopping from one foot to the other, uncertain and embarrassed.

Lottie risked a little smile. Hardly big enough to see, except with a magnifying glass.

Lisa smiled back, relieved.

Lottie held up the daisy chain she had just completed, and asked shyly, "Would you like it?"

Lisa dropped down beside her immediately. "Yes, but only if you put it on for me."

Lottie placed the flowers on Lisa's curls. Then she nodded. "Lovely," she said.

Now the doubles were sitting side by side on the grass, all alone, finding nothing to say, but smiling warily at each other.

Then Lisa took a deep breath and asked, "Are you still angry with me?"

Lottie shook her head.

Lisa looked at the ground. "It was so sudden," she said. "The bus! And then *you!* It was such a shock!"

Lottie nodded. "Such a shock," she repeated.

Lisa leaned forward. "But it's really fun when you get used to it, isn't it?"

Surprised, Lottie looked into her bright, merry eyes.

"Fun?" Then she asked softly, "Have you any brothers and sisters?"

"No."

"Neither have I," said Lottie.

"I have an idea," said Lisa. "Come on."

The two girls slipped away to the washroom and stood in front of a large mirror. Lottie tugged with a brush and comb at Lisa's curls.

Lisa cried, "Oh!" and "Ouch!"

"Will you keep quiet?" scolded Lottie, with pretended severity. "Do you always yell like that when your Mommy combs your hair?"

"I haven't got a Mommy," muttered Lisa. "That's why—*Ouch!*—that's why I'm such a tomboy, Daddy says."

"Doesn't he ever take a slipper to you?" inquired Lottie earnestly, as she began braiding Lisa's hair.

"Never! He's much too fond of me."

"That has nothing to do with it," observed Lottie, very wisely.

"And besides, he's got too many other things to do," Lisa added.

"It only takes one hand," Lottie retorted. Both girls laughed.

Then Lisa's braids were finished, and the two girls looked with eager eyes into the mirror. Their faces shone like Christmas trees. Two absolutely identical girls looked into the mirror. Two absolutely identical girls looked back out of it.

"Like two sisters!" whispered Lottie.

The midday gong sounded.

"This is going to be fun!" cried Lisa. "Come on!" As they ran out of the washroom, they were holding hands.

The other girls had taken their places long ago. Only Lisa's and Lottie's chairs were still unoccupied.

Then the door opened and Lottie appeared. Without hesitating she sat down in Lisa's place.

"Look out," warned Monica. "That's Lisa's place. Remember your shins."

Lottie shrugged and began to eat.

The door opened again and—bless my soul!—Lottie, Lottie in the flesh, came in a second time! Without looking around she went to the last unoccupied seat and sat down.

The other girls at the table opened their eyes and mouths. Those from the neighboring tables stared across and then jumped up from their seats and crowded around the two Lotties.

The tension did not relax until the two girls burst out laughing. Then the room suddenly echoed with many-voiced laughter.

Mrs. Muther frowned sternly. "What's all that noise about?" She rose and marched like an angry queen right into the thick of it. But when she saw both girls with braids, her wrath melted like snow in the sun. She was quite amused as she asked, "Now which of you is Lisa Palfy and which is Lottie Horn?"

"We're not going to tell you," said one Lottie, with a twinkle, and the treble laughter burst out again.

"Well, for goodness sake!" cried Mrs. Muther in comical despair. "What are we to do about it?"

"Perhaps," suggested the second Lottie cheerfully, "perhaps somebody can find out after all."

Steffie waved her hand in the air just as though she were back in school and knew the answer to a question. "I know!" she cried. "Trudie's in the same grade as Lisa at school. Trudie can tell us!"

Trudie pushed her way doubtfully into the foreground, looked carefully from one Lottie to the other, and shook her head helplessly. But then a roguish smile crossed her face. She took hold of one of the braids of the nearest Lottie and gave it a sharp tug. In a flash came the noise of a hearty slap.

Holding her check, Trudie shouted triumphantly, "That

was Lisa!" At which the general hilarity broke out louder than ever.

Right after lunch Lisa and Lottie were given permission to go down to the village. Their "doubleness" was to be fixed for all time by a camera, so that they could send home some pictures. What a surprise for their parents!

After recovering from his first astonishment, the photographer, a certain Mr. Appeldauer, worked with great efficiency. He took six separate photographs. The prints were to be ready in ten days.

When the two girls had gone, he said to his wife, "You know what I think I'll do? I'll send a few glossy prints to some of the big picture papers and magazines. They're often interested in things like that."

Safely outside, Lisa was undoing her "silly" braids, for that sober hair style imposed a certain strain upon her. When she could shake her curls freely, she really felt she was herself again. She invited Lottie to have a glass of lemonade. Lottie objected. Lisa said emphatically, "You must! The day before yesterday Daddy sent me some more pocket money. Come on!"

So they walked out to the house of the forester, who kept a little restaurant. They sat down at a table in the garden, drank lemonade, and talked. There were so many questions to ask.

The hens ran to and fro, pecking and clucking, between the tables. An old retriever came up to sniff the two children and found no objection to their remaining.

"Has your father been dead long?" asked Lisa.

"I don't know," said Lottie. "Mommy never mentions him."

Lisa nodded. "I can't remember my mother at all. There used to be a big photograph of her on Daddy's piano. But once he came in and caught me looking at it, and the next day it was gone. I think he locked it up in his desk."

The hens clucked. The retriever dozed. A little girl who had no father was drinking lemonade with a little girl who had no mother.

"You're nine too, aren't you?" asked Lisa.

"Yes," Lottie nodded. "I'll be ten on the fourteenth of October."

Lisa sat up as straight as a poker. "On the *fourteenth* of October?"

"On the fourteenth of October."

Lisa leaned forward and whispered, "So will I!"

Lottie went as stiff as an icicle.

A cock crowed beyond the house. The retriever snapped at a bee that was buzzing around him. Through the open kitchen window they could hear the forester's wife singing.

The two girls looked into each other's eyes as though hypnotized. Lottie swallowed hard and asked, hoarse with excitement, "And *where* were you born?"

Lisa answered in a low, hesitant voice, as though she were afraid. "At Linz on the Danube."

Lottie moistened her dry lips with her tongue. "So was I!"

In the garden all was still. Only the tips of the trees were moving.

Lottie said slowly, "I have a picture of—of my Mommy in my locker."

Lisa jumped up. "Show it to me!" She dragged Lottie from her chair and out of the garden.

"Wait!" shouted an angry voice. "What's the idea!" It was the forester's wife. "Drinking lemonade and going off without paying!"

With trembling fingers Lisa rummaged in her purse, pressed a coin into the woman's hand, and ran back to Lottie.

"What about the change?" shouted the woman. But the two children did not hear. They were running as fast as they could.

"Now where are those young monkeys off to?" muttered the forester's wife. She went back into the house, and the old retriever trotted after her.

Back at the camp, Lottie hurriedly searched her locker. She dug the photograph out from under a pile of clothes and held it out to Lisa, who was jumping with eagerness.

Lisa took one shy, frightened glance at the picture. Then her face brightened, and her eyes stayed firmly fixed on the face of the woman in the picture.

Lottie watched Lisa expectantly.

Exhausted with sheer happiness, Lisa lowered the photograph and nodded blissfully. Then she hugged it passionately, and whispered, "My Mommy! It's the same picture!"

Lottie put her arms around Lisa's neck. "*Our* Mommy!" Two little girls clung tightly to each other.

The gong boomed through the house. Children ran laughing and shouting down the stairs. Lisa started to put the photograph back in the locker, but Lottie said, "You can keep it."

Miss Ursula was standing before the desk in Mrs. Muther's office. She was so excited that on both her cheeks were round spots, red as apples.

"I *can't* keep it to myself!" she blurted out. "I *must* confide in you. If only I knew what we ought to do!"

"Come, come," said Mrs. Muther. "What have you got on your mind, my dear?"

"They are *not* astrological twins."

"Who aren't?" asked Mrs. Muther with a smile. "King Edward and the tailor?"

"No! Lisa Palfy and Lottie Horn! I've checked back in our registration book. They were both born on the same day of the same year at Linz. It simply *cannot* be a coincidence."

"I don't think it's a coincidence either, my dear. In fact, I have some ideas of my own on the subject."

"So you know?" asked Miss Ursula, panting for breath.

"Of course. When little Lottie arrived, I got her date and place of birth and entered them in the book. Then I compared them with Lisa's. That was the obvious thing to do, wasn't it?"

"Yes, yes. But what do we do now?"

"Nothing."

"Nothing?"

"Nothing! If you don't keep quiet about it, I'll—I don't know what I'll do to you!"

"But—"

"There's no 'but.' The two children suspect nothing. They have just been photographed together, and they'll send the pictures home. If that helps to unravel the knot, well and good. But as for you and me, we'll not interfere. Thank you for your sympathetic understanding, my dear. And now, please, will you ask the cook to come in and see me?"

*New worlds are discovered • Mystery piled
on mystery • The bisected first name • A serious
photograph and a funny letter • Can
children be cut in half?*

Time passed.

The two girls collected their photographs from Mr. Appeldauer. The inquisitive Miss Ursula inquired whether they had sent the pictures home. Lisa and Lottie nodded their heads and said yes.

But the pictures, torn into little pieces, are at the bottom of Lake Bohren. The two girls told Miss Ursula a lie. They wanted to keep their secret to themselves. They lied shamelessly to anyone who tried to pry too closely into their affairs. Their consciences did not prick them—not even Lottie's.

The two girls stuck together like burrs. Trudie, Steffie, Monica, Christine, and the rest were sometimes angry at Lisa and jealous of Lottie. What good did it do? None at all!

They had slipped off to the locker room. Lottie looked through her locker, took out two identical sweaters, gave one to her sister, and put on the other herself.

"Mommy bought these," she said, "at Pollinger's."

"Ah!" exclaimed Lisa. "That's the store in Neuhauser Street, near—what is the name of that gate?"

"Carl's Gate."

"That's right—near Carl's Gate."

By now they were well informed about each other's way of life, school friends, neighbors, teachers, and apartments. For Lisa, everything connected with her mother was terribly important. And Lottie longed to know everything—*any* little thing—that her sister could tell her about her father. For days on end they talked of nothing else. And in bed at night they whispered together for hours. It was as though they were each discovering a new and strange continent. They had found out that what they had known up to now was only half a world.

And at moments when they were not fitting together these two halves in order to get a glimpse of the whole, another subject excited them, another mystery tormented them: why were their parents no longer together?

"First, of course, they got married," said Lisa for the hundredth time. "Then they had us. And they named me Lisa and you Lottie because Mommy's name is Lisalottie. That's pretty, isn't it? They must have been fond of each other in those days, mustn't they?"

"I'm sure of it," said Lottie. "And then they must have quarreled and parted. And they separated us just the same as they separated Mommy's first name."

"They really ought to have asked us first."

"But when that happened we probably hadn't even learned to talk."

The two sisters smiled. Then they linked arms and went into the garden.

The mail had come. Everywhere—in the grass, on the wall, and on the garden benches—campers were sitting, studying letters.

Lottie held in her hands the photograph of a man of about thirty-five. She was looking with loving eyes at her father. So that was how he looked! And this was the sort of feeling you had around your heart when you had a real live father!

Lisa read aloud what he had written to her. " '*My dearest, only child*'—what a liar!" she said, looking up. "He knows perfectly well he has twins!" She went on reading:

I think you must have completely forgotten what your old father looks like. Otherwise you wouldn't be so anxious for a photograph of him just before the end of your vacation. At first I thought I would send you a picture of me as a baby—one that shows me lying on a polar-bear skin. But you wrote that it must be an absolutely brandnew one. So I rushed off to the photographer's, though I really couldn't spare the time, and explained to him just why I needed it in such a hurry. I told him that unless he took my picture my Lisa wouldn't recognize me when I went to the station to meet her. Fortunately he saw how

*important it was. And so you're getting it in good time.
I'm sorry for the counselors there. I hope you don't lead
them such a dance as you do your father—who sends you
a thousand kisses and is longing to have you home again.*

"Lovely!" said Lottie. "And funny! And yet in the picture
he looks quite serious."

"He was probably too shy to laugh in front of the photographer," Lisa speculated. "He always looks serious in front of
other people. But when we're alone we have lots of fun."

Lottie hugged the picture. "May I really keep it?"

"Of course," said Lisa. "That's why I got him to send it."

Steffie was sitting on a bench with a letter in her hands, crying. She wasn't making a sound, but the tears streamed steadily
down her round little cheeks.

Trudie sauntered by, stopped curiously, went and sat down
by Steffie, and looked at her expectantly.

Christine came up and sat down on the other side of Steffie.

Lisa and Lottie approached and stopped. "What's wrong,
Steffie?" asked Lisa.

Steffie continued to cry silently. Suddenly she looked down
and said in a flat voice, "My Mommy and Daddy are going to
be divorced."

"What a mean thing!" cried Trudie. "They send you off to
camp, and then do a thing like that—behind your back!"

"I think Daddy wants to marry somebody else," sobbed
Steffie.

Lisa and Lottie walked away quickly. What they had just heard had stirred them to the depths.

"*Our* father," said Lottie, "hasn't got a new wife, has he?"

"No," returned Lisa. "I'd know if he had."

"Maybe there's someone he's planning to marry?" asked Lottie hesitantly.

Lisa shook her curly head. "Of course he has a lot of friends. Women friends, too. But I know he's not planning to marry. But what about Mommy? Has she a—a man friend?"

"No," said Lottie confidently. "Mommy has me and her work, and that's all she asks of life, she says."

Lisa gave her sister a puzzled look. "Why do you suppose they got divorced?"

Lottie thought for a while. "I wonder if they ever really went to court. I mean, like Steffie's father and mother."

"If they didn't, why is Daddy in Vienna and Mommy in Munich?" asked Lisa. "Why did they separate us?"

"Why," went on Lottie broodingly, "didn't they ever tell us that we were really twins? And why has Daddy never told you that Mommy's still living?"

"Mommy's never told you that Daddy's still living, either." Lisa put her hands on her hips and stuck out her elbows. "Fine parents we've got, haven't we? Just wait till we tell them a few things! That'll make them sit up!"

"We couldn't do that," said Lottie timidly. "We're only children."

"*Only!*" laughed Lisa and tossed her head.

*Stuffed pancakes, how horrid! • The
mysterious little notebooks • A conspiracy
is afoot • Dress rehearsal • Good-by to
Bohrlaken on Lake Bohren!*

Vacation was coming to an end. The piles of clean clothes had
been put in the trunks. The children scarcely knew whether
to be sad at leaving or happy at the prospect of returning
home.

Mrs. Muther was planning a garden party. The father of
one of the girls owned a big store, and he had sent a packing
case full of Chinese lanterns, colored streamers, and the like.
Now counselors and children together were hard at work
decorating the veranda and the garden. They lugged step-
ladders from tree to tree, hung the gaudy lanterns among
the foliage, looped the crepe paper streamers from bough to
bough, and fixed up, on a long table, a handsome box from
which lucky numbers would be drawn for prizes. Others wrote
numbers on slips of paper. The first prize was a beautiful pair
of roller skates.

"Where have Curls and Braids gone?" asked Miss Ursula.

(Such were her new names for Lisa and Lottie.)

"Oh, *them!*" said Monica, scornfully. "They're probably sitting in the grass somewhere, holding hands so that the wind won't blow them apart."

The twins were not sitting in the grass somewhere, but in the garden at the forester's restaurant. Nor were they holding hands—they had no time for such things. Each had a little notebook in front of her, and a pencil in her hand, and at that moment Lottie was dictating to the industriously scribbling Lisa, "Mommy's favorite dish is beef stew with noodles. You go to Huber's and get half a pound of the best lean beef for stewing."

Lisa looked up. "Huber, family butcher, corner of Max Emanuel Street and Prince Eugene Street," she recited.

Lottie nodded approvingly. "The cook book is in the kitchen cupboard on the left-hand side of the bottom shelf, and it has in it all the recipes I know."

Lisa wrote down: *Cook book — kitchen cupboard — bottom shelf at left*. Then she dropped the pencil and rested her chin in her hands. "I'm scared stiff of cooking," she said. "But if anything goes wrong in the first few days, I can say I've forgotten how to do it while I was away for vacation."

Lottie nodded doubtfully. "After all, you can write me at once if things go wrong. I'll go to the post office every day to see if there's a letter for me."

"So will I," said Lisa. "Don't forget to write often. And

you'll have some wonderful meals at the Imperial. Daddy's always so pleased when I eat a lot."

"What a pity stuffed pancakes are your favorite dish," complained Lottie. "Well, it can't be helped. But I'd much rather have veal cutlet or goulash."

"If you eat three pancakes the first day, or four or five, you can say you've had enough to last you the rest of your life," suggested Lisa.

"Yes, I might do that," answered her sister. But the very thought of five pancakes made her stomach turn over.

Then the two girls bent over their notebooks again, and repeated over and over to each other the names of classmates, their marks in different subjects, bits of information about their teachers, and the quickest way to school.

"It's going to be easier for you to go to school than for me," said Lisa. "All you have to do is ask Trudie to call for you the first morning. She stops by for me sometimes. And then you just let her take the lead, while you learn what the streets look like and all the rest of it."

Lottie nodded. Then she gave a start. "Goodness, there's something I forgot to tell you! Don't forget to kiss Mommy when she comes to say good night to you."

Lisa looked at her sister. "I don't need to write that down," she said. "I'm not likely to forget *that!*"

The twins had decided not to tell their parents that they knew the truth. They couldn't be sure how their parents would react to the news. They dreaded the possibility of decisions that might destroy their chance for happiness together in the future. But still less could they bring themselves to take the other course—to go back to the homes they had left as though nothing had happened.

In short, a conspiracy was afoot. . . . They would exchange clothes, hair styles, trunks, toys, characters, and private lives! Curly-haired Lisa would go "home" with tidy braids and the determination to be tidy in other ways too, just as though she were Lottie—home to the mother she knew only through a photograph. And Lottie would comb out her braids into long curls and go to her father in Vienna, determined to be as merry and lively as she knew how.

They made the most careful preparations for their future adventures. The little notebooks were chock-full. They did not dare risk addressing letters to each other at home, but agreed to write through General Delivery in case of a crisis, or if anything important or unexpected should happen.

Perhaps by keeping a sharp lookout they would finally unravel the mystery of why their parents were living apart. And perhaps one fine, one glorious day, they would live with each other and with both parents. But they scarcely dared think, much less speak, of anything so wonderful and so uncertain.

They decided to make the garden party, on the eve of their departure, a dress rehearsal. Lottie appeared as the curly-headed, high-spirited Lisa. Lisa came with braids as the demure Lottie. And both played their parts to perfection. No one had the least idea of the truth! Not even Trudie, Lisa's friend from Vienna. Each of them found it thrilling to call out to the other by her own name. Lottie was so excited that she turned somersaults, and Lisa was so gentle and quiet that you would have thought she couldn't say "boo" to a goose and butter wouldn't melt in her mouth.

The Chinese lanterns gleamed among the summer leaves. The streamers swayed in the evening breeze. Party and vacation were both coming to an end. The lucky numbers had all been pulled from the box on the long table, and Steffie had drawn the first prize—the roller skates.

At last, still playing their parts, the two girls were asleep in each other's beds, dreaming strange, excited dreams. Lottie, for instance, was met at the station in Vienna by a more than life-sized photograph of her father, and standing beside him was a cook in a tall white hat, with a huge tray full of steaming stuffed pancakes—ugh!

Next morning, at the crack of dawn, two trains coming from opposite directions steamed into the station at Egern, near Bohrlaken on Lake Bohren. Dozens of little girls climbed chattering into the cars.

Lottie leaned out of the window. From a window of the other train Lisa waved to her. They smiled to give each other courage. Their hearts were thumping, they were growing more and more nervous. If the engines had not begun to hiss and spit at that moment . . .

But no! The timetable decided otherwise. The stationmaster waved his flag. Both trains began to move. The children waved.

Lottie was going as Lisa to Vienna.

Lisa was going as Lottie to Munich.

*The girl on the trunk • Lonely uncles • Peterkin
and the unfailing instinct of animals • "Lisa"
at the Opera • Mistakes in a housekeeping
book • Mr. Palfy's complex inner life*

The main station at Munich. Platform 16. The engine came
to a halt and gasped for breath. Islands of reunion formed
in the sea of travelers. Little girls hugged their beaming parents. Happy and excited with the flood of greetings, people
forgot they were in the station and acted as though they were
already at home.

But gradually the platform emptied.

And at last there was only one little girl left, a girl with
braids tied in ribbons. Up to yesterday she had had curls. Up
to yesterday her name had been Lisa Palfy.

At last she settled down on her trunk to wait at the station
in a strange town; to wait for her mother whom she had never
seen except in a photograph.

Mrs. Lisalottie Palfy, who had been Lisalottie Horn before
she married, had resumed her maiden name after her divorce

seven and a half years ago. She was now held up at the office of the *Munich Illustrated* where she worked as picture editor. Some new photographs had just come in for the next issue.

At last she managed to grab a taxi. At last she struggled through the big, crowded station to platform 16.

Way off at the far end she saw a child, sitting on a trunk. The young woman flashed down the platform like a fire engine.

The knees of the little girl huddled on the trunk were trembling. A feeling she had never known welled up in her heart. That real, radiant, living, flashing young woman was her mother!

"Mommy!" Lisa ran towards her, held out her arms, and threw them around her mother's neck.

"My little housekeeper!" whispered the young woman, with tears in her eyes. "At last, at last I've got you back!"

The little girl could hardly stop kissing her mother's shining face, her soft hair, her little hat. Yes, even the hat!

Up in the restaurant and down in the kitchen of the Hotel Imperial there was benevolent excitement. A little girl, favorite of all regular customers and of the staff, daughter of Mr. Palfy, conductor at the Opera House, had come home from camp.

Lottie—no—*Lisa* was in her usual place, her chair with the two big cushions, eating stuffed pancakes as though her life depended on it.

The regular customers came over to the table one by one, stroked the little girl's curly hair, patted her gently on the shoulder, asked how she had enjoyed herself, remarked that after all no place could be nicer than Vienna with Daddy here, put all kinds of presents on the table—gumdrops, chocolates, pralines, colored pencils. One even took from his pocket a little old-fashioned needlecase and observed awkwardly that it had been the property of his late grandmother. Then they nodded to Mr. Palfy the conductor and went back to their tables. Today they were really going to enjoy lunch again, poor lonely "uncles!"

But no one had a better appetite than Mr. Palfy himself. He had always strongly emphasized the need of "all true artists" to be alone; he had always thought his marriage a mistake, a step into the humdrum middle-class world; but today he was experiencing a warm family feeling that was most "inartistic." And when his daughter took his hand with a shy smile, as though to prevent his running away, then, even though he wasn't eating Irish stew, he felt something like a dumpling in his throat.

Franz, the waiter, came waddling up with another pancake.

Lottie shook her curls. "I couldn't possibly, Mr. Franz!"

"But Lisa!" cried the waiter reproachfully. "It's only the fifth!"

When the puzzled Franz had waddled back to the kitchen with the fifth pancake, Lottie plucked up her courage. "Do you know, Daddy," she said, "in the future I'm always going to have the same food as you."

"You don't say!" cried Mr. Palfy. "But how about when I eat smoked ham? You know you can't stand smoked ham. It makes you feel sick."

"When you eat smoked ham," she said miserably, "I'll have pancakes again." Sometimes it is not quite so easy being your own sister!

Just then Dr. Strobel appeared with Peterkin, his dog. "Look, Peterkin," said the doctor with a smile. "See who's here! Go and say how-do-you-do to Lisa."

Peterkin wagged his tail and trotted quickly up to the Palfys' table to say how-do-you-do to his old friend Lisa.

When Peterkin arrived at the table, he sniffed at the little

girl, turned around, and quickly trotted back to his master.

"What a stupid dog!" Dr. Strobel complained. "Can't even recognize his best friend! Just because she's been away in the country for a week or two. And people talk a lot of nonsense about the unfailing instinct of animals!"

But Lottie thought to herself, "What a good thing that doctors are not as clever as dogs!"

After dinner Mr. Palfy, his daughter, the trunk, the presents, a doll, and a beach-bag containing Lottie's bathing suits returned to his apartment in Rotenturm Street. And Rosa, Mr. Palfy's housekeeper, was beside herself with joy at seeing the child again.

But Lottie knew from what Lisa had told her that Rosa was a two-faced cat and was merely putting on an act. Daddy, of course, did not notice it.

He fished a ticket out of his wallet and gave it to his daughter. "This evening I'm conducting Humperdinck's *Hänsel and Gretel*," he said. "Rosa will bring you to the Opera House and take you home again at the end of the performance."

"Oh!" Lottie beamed. "Can I see you from where I'm sitting?"

"Certainly you can."

"And will you look at me sometimes?"

"Of course."

"And may I give a little wave when you look at me?"

"Yes, and I'll wave back to you, Lisa."

Then the telephone rang. A feminine voice was speaking from the other end. Lottie's father made very brief replies, but when he put down the receiver he seemed to be in rather a hurry. He had to be alone for a few hours. Yes, a composition, for he was not only a conductor, but also a composer.

And he simply *could not* compose at home. He did his composing in a studio in Ring Street, which he had taken expressly for the purpose. So . . .

"I'll see you at lunch tomorrow at the Imperial."

"And I may wave to you in the Opera House, Daddy?"

"Of course, my dear. Why not?"

A kiss on the grave child's forehead.

The door slammed.

The little girl walked slowly to the window and thought sadly about life. They wouldn't *let* her mother work at home; and her father *couldn't* work at home. What a handful parents are!

But since she was a determined and practical little girl—largely on account of her mother's training—she soon dropped these gloomy reflections. She armed herself with her little notebook and with the help of Lisa's instructions began a voyage of discovery through that fine apartment in old Vienna.

When she had completed her investigation, she sat down as usual to look over the housekeeping account book that lay there on the kitchen table, and worked one by one through the columns of expenses.

In doing so she noticed two things: first, that Rosa the housekeeper had made a mistake on practically every page, and second, that every one of these mistakes was to Rosa's advantage.

"Well! What does this mean?" Rosa was standing in the kitchen door.

"I've been adding up the figures in your book," said Lottie, in a low but firm voice.

"What gave you that idea?" cried Rosa indignantly. "You do your arithmetic in school. That's the place for it."

"I shall always add up your books," declared Lottie, and hopped off the kitchen chair. "We learn *in* school, but not *for* school—that's what my teacher says." And with that, she stalked out of the room.

Rosa looked after her, flabbergasted.

But there was still so much to be learned about the past. Lottie's father, Arnold Palfy, was a musician, and artists are well known to be strange beings. He did not wear a broad-brimmed hat or a flapping tie. On the contrary, he was very well dressed.

But when he had an idea for a composition he found it absolutely essential to go away immediately and be alone, so that he could note it down and develop it. Such an idea might come when he was at a party. "What's become of Palfy?" his host would ask. And somebody would answer, "He's probably had an idea!" And his host would answer, "What manners! A man can't run away whenever he gets an idea!" But Mr. Palfy could, and did.

He even used to run out of his own apartment when he was just married.

And then, when the little twins howled day and night in the apartment, and the Vienna Philharmonic Orchestra was about to give the first performance of his first piano concerto, he simply had his grand piano carted away and installed in a studio on Ring Street. He had taken the studio in desperation in order to be able to write his musical compositions.

Lisalottie Palfy, who had been Lisalottie Horn, barely twenty years of age, did not find it very cheerful. She grew desperate and sued for divorce.

And so Conductor Palfy could now be alone as much as he liked. He engaged a capable nurse in Rotenturm Street to look after the one twin left to him after the divorce. And as he had so earnestly desired, not a soul bothered him.

But soon that did not suit him either. All the same, he went on composing and conducting and grew more famous year by year. And he could always go to his apartment in Rotenturm Street and play with his baby daughter Lisa.

Whenever there was a concert in Munich at which a new work by Arnold Palfy was being played, Lisalottie Horn bought herself a ticket and sat in one of the cheap seats at the back, and learned from her ex-husband's music that he had not grown any happier. In spite of his success . . . and in spite of being alone.

*You can't unlearn how to cook • Lottie at the
opera • Showers of pralines • The first
night in Munich and in Vienna • A curious
dream • Forget-me-not, Munich 18*

Mrs. Lisalottie Horn just had time to take her daughter home
to her tiny apartment in Max Emanuel Street and rush back,
at full speed and very willingly, to her office.

Lisa—no—*Lottie* took a first careful look around the apartment. Then she collected the keys, her mother's purse, and a
net bag, and set out to do the shopping.

At Huber's the butcher on the corner of Prince Eugene
Street, she bought half a pound of the best lean beef for
stewing, a beef kidney, and a few marrowbones. Then she
looked around desperately for Mrs. Wagental's grocery, where
she wanted to buy mixed herbs, noodles, and salt.

Annie Habersetzer was not a little surprised to catch sight
of her schoolmate Lottie Horn standing in the middle of the
road, anxiously turning the pages of a notebook.

"Do you do your homework in the street?" she asked
curiously. "Don't you know vacation isn't over yet?"

Lisa stared at her in bewilderment. It is maddening to be spoken to by someone you are supposed to know well, whom you have never seen before in your life! Finally she pulled herself together and said brightly, "Hello! Come with me. I've got to go to Mrs. Wagental's for some mixed herbs." Then she put her arm through that of the strange girl—and let her unconsciously pilot her to Mrs. Wagental's store.

Mrs. Wagental was naturally glad to see Lottie Horn back from her vacation, and with such red cheeks, too! When Lisa had bought what she wanted, Mrs. Wagental gave each of the girls a piece of candy and asked them to remember her kindly to Mrs. Horn and Mrs. Habersetzer.

That took a load off Lisa's mind. At last she knew that the other girl was Annie Habersetzer. (This is what the notebook said about her: *Annie Habersetzer—I've had a row with her three times. She bullies the smaller girls, especially Elsa Merck, who is the smallest girl in the class.*) Well, that was enough to start with.

When they parted outside her house, Lisa said, "And that reminds me, Annie. We've quarreled three times already about the way you treat Elsa Merck. You know what I mean. Next time I won't just *talk* to you, I'll—" And with that she made an unmistakable motion with her hand and ran off.

"We'll see about that," thought Annie furiously. "We'll see about it in the morning. She must have gone crazy during vacation."

Lisa was cooking. She had put on one of Mommy's aprons, and was spinning to and fro like a top between the gas stove, where the saucepans were boiling, and the table, on which lay the open cook book. Every few minutes she lifted a saucepan lid. When the water hissed and boiled over, she jumped. How much salt should she put in the noodles? "Half a teaspoonful!" How much celery salt? "A pinch!" How much, for goodness sake, is a pinch? And then, "Grate a nutmeg." Where were the nutmegs? Where was the grater?

She rummaged in drawers, climbed on chairs, looked into all the canisters, glanced at the clock on the wall. She jumped down from a chair, grabbed a fork, lifted a lid, burned her fingers, squealed, stabbed the beef with the fork—no, it wasn't done yet.

She stood stock-still, holding the fork in her hand. What was she looking for? Oh, yes, the nutmeg and grater. Goodness! What was that lying so quietly beside the cook book? The mixed herbs! They had to be cleaned and put in the broth! Down with the fork, up with the knife. Was the meat done yet? And where were the gratemeg and the nutter? Oh, dear, the grater and the nutmeg? First the herbs had to be washed under the tap, and then the carrots had to be scraped. Ouch! You had to watch out that you didn't cut yourself! And when the meat was done, you had to take it from the saucepan and drain off the liquid. For that you needed a colander. And

Mommy would be here in half an hour! And twenty minutes before she arrived you had to drop the noodles in boiling water. What a mess the kitchen was in! And the nutmeg! And the colander! And the grater! And . . . and . . . and . . .

Lisa flopped down on a kitchen chair. Oh, Lottie! It's not so easy being your own sister! Hotel Imperial . . . Dr. Strobel . . . Peterkin . . . Franz . . . And Daddy . . . Daddy . . . Daddy . . .

The clock ticked on.

In twenty-nine minutes Mommy would be here! . . . In twenty-eight and a half minutes! . . . In twenty-eight minutes . . .

Lisa clenched her fists in determination and got up to start again. As she did so, she growled to herself, "If I can't manage this . . ."

But that's the queer thing about cooking. Determination is all very well if you want to jump off a tower. But will power is not enough when it comes to cooking beef and noodles.

And when Mrs. Horn came home, tired with a day's exertions, she did not find a smiling little housekeeper awaiting her. Not at all. She found a completely exhausted scrap of misery, a slightly damaged, confused, crumpled little object, from whose mouth, twisted ready for tears, came the words, "Mommy, don't be angry! I think I've unlearned how to cook."

"But Lottie, you can't unlearn how to cook," cried her mother, surprised. But there was not much time for surprise. There were tears to dry. There was broth to taste, overcooked meat to add to it, plates and knives and forks to be brought from the cupboard, and many other things to do.

When at last they were sitting under the lamp in the living room, eating their beef and noodle soup, Mrs. Horn said comfortingly, "It tastes all right in spite of everything, doesn't it?"

"Does it?" A timid smile stole across her daughter's face. "Does it, really?"

Her mother nodded and smiled back reassuringly.

Lisa breathed again. And now suddenly the food really tasted better than anything she had ever eaten in her life. Not even excepting the Hotel Imperial and the stuffed pancakes.

"I'll do the cooking myself for a day or two," said her mother. "You can watch me. Then you'll soon be as good as you were before camp."

Lisa nodded vigorously. "Perhaps even better," she said, with a touch of sauciness.

After the meal they washed the dishes together, and Lisa told her mother what a grand time she had had at camp. But she did not breathe a word about the other girl who was the living image of herself.

Meanwhile Lottie, in Lisa's prettiest frock, was sitting pressed close to the plush front of a dress-circle box at the Vienna Opera House, looking down with shining eyes at the orchestra, where Mr. Palfy was conducting the overture to *Hänsel and Gretel.*

How wonderful Daddy looked in evening clothes! And how well the musicians obeyed him, although there were some quite old gentlemen among them. When he made masterful, threatening movements with his baton, they played as loud as a thunderstorm. And when he wanted them to play softly, they made sounds as gentle as an evening breeze. How frightened they must be of him! And yet a few minutes ago, when he waved up at the box, he had looked so kind and friendly. It was hard to believe he was the same man.

The door of the box opened.

A beautifully gowned young lady swept in, sat down near the front, and smiled at Lottie as the child looked up.

Lottie turned away shyly and went on watching her Daddy conduct the orchestra.

The young lady produced a pair of opera glasses. And a box of pralines. And a program. And a compact. She went on producing things until the plush railing in front of the box was like a shop window.

At the end of the overture the audience clapped loudly. Conductor Palfy bowed repeatedly. And then, as he lifted his baton again, he looked up at the box.

Lottie waved her hand shyly. This time Daddy smiled even more sweetly than before.

And then Lottie noticed that she was not the only one waving. The lady at her side was waving, too.

Was she waving to Daddy? Was it possible that Daddy had smiled so sweetly at the young lady? And not at his little daughter? And why had Lisa never told her about this strange woman? Had Daddy met her only recently? Lottie made a mental note: *Write to Lisa tonight. Ask if she knows anything. Mail it tomorrow on the way to school. Address—General Delivery, Forget-me-not, Munich 18.*

Then the curtain rose, and the fate of Hänsel and Gretel called for all her attention. Lottie held her breath. Down on the stage the parents were sending their children into the forest to get rid of them. And yet they were fond of them!

How could they be so wicked? Or were they? Was it only *what they were doing* that was wicked? If it made them so unhappy, why did they do it?

Lottie, the substituted twin, grew more and more agitated. Though she was not fully aware of it, her emotions were concerned less and less with the two children and their parents down there on the stage, and more and more with herself, her twin sister, and her own parents. Had they the right to do what they had done? Mommy was not in the least wicked; neither was Daddy. Yet what they had *done*—that *was* wicked. The woodman and his wife were so poor that they could not buy food for their children. But Daddy? Had Daddy ever been poor?

Later, when Hänsel and Gretel arrived outside the gingerbread house, picked pieces off the walls, and were startled by the voice of the witch, Miss Irene Gerlach—for that was the elegant young lady's name—leaned over to Lottie, pushed the box of pralines towards her, and whispered, "Would you like something to nibble, too?"

Lottie jumped, looked up, saw the woman's face close to hers, and threw out her hand in self-defense. And her hand hit the box of candy, knocking it off the plush railing. A shower of pralines rained on the seats below! Heads turned and looked up. Suppressed laughter mingled with the music. Miss Gerlach smiled, half embarrassed, half annoyed.

Lottie went stiff with fright. "I beg your pardon," she murmured.

The lady smiled forgiveness. "It doesn't matter, Lisa," she said.

Perhaps she was a witch. A more beautiful witch than the one on the stage.

Lisa was lying in bed in Munich for the first time. Her mother was sitting on the edge of the bed. "There, Lottie dear," she said. "Sleep well! And pleasant dreams!"

"If I'm not too tired," murmured Lisa. "You won't be long, will you?"

There was a larger bed by the opposite wall. On the turned-back bedspread was Mommy's nightgown, ready to slip into.

"I'm coming," said her mother, "as soon as you're asleep."

Lisa threw her arms around her mother's neck and gave her a kiss. Then another, and another. "Good night!"

The young woman hugged her little daughter. "I'm so happy to have you back," she said softly. "You're all I have now!"

Lisa's head sank back sleepily. Lisalottie Horn tucked in the bedclothes and listened for a while to her daughter's breathing. Then she rose quietly and tiptoed back into the living room.

Her brief case lay there under the lamp. She still had a great deal to do.

Lottie had gone to bed for the first time under the eye of sulky Rosa. Soon afterwards she stealthily got up again and wrote the letter she intended to drop in the mailbox early the next morning. Then she got quietly back into Lisa's bed and, before switching off the light, examined her bedroom again at her leisure.

It was a large, attractive room with fairy-tale figures around the walls, a cupboard for toys, a bookcase, a desk for doing homework, a big toy grocery shop, a graceful, old-fashioned dressing table, a doll's carriage, and a doll's bed. Nothing was missing except the one thing that mattered.

Had she not sometimes—quite secretly, so that Mommy would not suspect—wished for just such a beautiful room as this? And now that she had it, a sharp pain, pointed with envy and longing, bored into her heart. She longed for the modest little bedroom where her sister was now lying, for Mommy's good-night kiss, for the beam of light under the door of the living room; for the sound of that door quietly opening, of Mommy's stopping beside her bed, stepping on tiptoe over to her own bed, slipping into her nightie, and snuggling down between the sheets.

If only Daddy's bed were here, or at least in the *next* room! Perhaps he would snore. That would be wonderful. Then she would know that he was near. But he was not near; he was sleeping in another place—in Ring Street. Perhaps he wasn't even there. Perhaps he was sitting with the stylish praline-lady in a great, glittering room, laughing and dancing with her, nodding affectionately to her as he had done at the opera—to *her,* not to his little daughter, who had waved so happily to him from the box.

Lottie fell asleep. She had a dream. The story of the poor father and mother who sent Hänsel and Gretel into the forest because they had no food for them became entangled with her own fears and unhappiness.

Lottie and Lisa were sitting—in the dream—on the same bed, staring with terrified eyes at a door through which many bakers in white caps entered, carrying loaves of bread. They piled up the loaves against the walls. More and more bakers came and went. The piles of loaves grew higher. The room got smaller and smaller.

Then her father was standing there in his evening clothes, conducting the parade of bakers with lively movements. Mommy came rushing in and asked anxiously, "But Arnold, what's going to happen now?"

"We must send the children away!" he shouted angrily. "There's no more room for them. There are too many loaves in the house!"

Mommy wrung her hands. The children sobbed wretchedly.

"Get out!" he cried and raised his conductor's baton threateningly. Then the bed rolled obediently to the window. The window flew open. The bed floated out.

It flew over a big city, across a river, over hills, fields, mountains, and forests. Then it dipped back to earth again and landed in a great thicket of trees, like a primitive forest, which reverberated frighteningly with the uncanny croaking of birds and the roaring of wild beasts. The two little girls sat up in bed, paralyzed with fear.

There was a rustling and crackling in the thicket.

The children threw themselves down and pulled the bed-clothes over their heads. And then the witch came out of the underbrush. But it was not the witch who was on the stage of the Opera House; she looked much more like the praline-lady in the box. She surveyed the bed through her opera glasses, nodded her head, smiled very haughtily, and clapped her hands three times.

As though at a word of command, the dark wood was trans-formed into a sunny meadow. And in the meadow was a house built of praline boxes, with a fence consisting of bars of choco-late. Birds twittered gaily, taffy rabbits hopped about in the grass, and all around were shining, golden nests full of Easter eggs. A little bird alighted on the bed and sang such pretty trills that Lottie and Lisa came out from under the bedclothes, though at first only as far as the tips of their noses. When they saw the meadow with the taffy rabbits, the chocolate eggs, and the praline-box house, they jumped quickly out of bed and ran to the fence. There they stood in amazement in their long nightgowns. "Special mixture!" read Lisa aloud. "With nuts! And nougat centers!"

"And lemon drops, too!" cried Lottie delightedly. For even in her dreams she did not care for sickly sweets.

Lisa broke a large piece of chocolate from the fence.

"Almonds!" she said greedily and raised it to her lips.

At that the witch's laughter echoed from the house. The children started. Lisa threw the chocolate away.

And then Mommy came, panting across the meadow with a large wheelbarrow full of loaves of bread.

"Stop, children!" she cried in horror. "It's all poisoned!"

"We were so hungry, Mommy!"

"Here are loaves of bread for you. I couldn't get away from the office any earlier." She threw her arms around them and tried to drag them away. But suddenly the door of the praline-box house opened. Daddy appeared with a big saw such as woodcutters use and shouted, "Leave the children alone, Mrs. Horn!"

"They are *my* children, Mr. Palfy!"

"Mine *too*," he shouted back. And, as he came towards them, he explained, "I'll cut the children in half. With the saw! I get half of Lottie and half of Lisa, and you get the same, Mrs. Horn!"

The trembling twins jumped back into bed.

Mommy spread out her arms and stood protectively in front of the bed. "Never, Mr. Palfy!"

But Daddy pushed her aside and began, starting at the head of the bed, to saw through it. The saw shrieked in a way to freeze your blood, and moved inch by inch down the length of the bed.

"Let go of each other's hands," Daddy ordered.

The saw came nearer and nearer to the intertwined hands

of the two sisters, nearer and still nearer. It was on the point of slicing the flesh.

Mommy cried broken-heartedly.

They could hear the witch chuckling.

Then the children's hands let go.

The saw cut down between them till the bed was sawed completely in two and became two beds, each with four legs.

"Which twin will you have, Mrs. Horn?"

"Both! Both!"

"Sorry," said the man. "We have to be fair. Well, if you can't make up your mind, I'll have this one. I don't care which. I can't tell them apart, anyhow." He seized one of the beds. "Which one are you?"

"Lisa!" she cried. "But you can't do it!"

"No!" screamed Lottie. "You can't separate us!"

"Be still," he said sternly. "Parents can do as they like." With that, he walked towards the praline-box house, dragging the bed behind him on a string. The chocolate fence opened of its own accord.

Lisa and Lottie waved to each other despairingly.

"We'll write!" shouted Lisa.

"General Delivery!" shouted Lottie. "Forget-me-not, Munich 18!"

Daddy and Lisa disappeared into the house. Then the house itself vanished, as though it had been wiped out.

Mommy threw her arms around Lottie. "Now we two are all forlorn," she said sadly. Suddenly she stared doubtfully at

Lottie. "Which of my daughters are you? You look like Lottie."

"I *am* Lottie!"

"No, you look like Lisa . . ."

"I *am* Lisa!"

Mommy looked into her daughter's eyes with a startled expression, and said, speaking somehow in Daddy's voice, "Now curls, now braids! The same heads, the same noses!"

And then Lottie had a braid on the left side of her head and curls like Lisa's on the right. The tears streamed down her cheeks. And she said wretchedly, "Now I don't know which of the two I am. Oh, poor half, poor me!"

*Peterkin adjusts himself • Everything is different,
especially Rosa • Conductor Palfy gives piano
lessons • Annie Habersetzer gets her comeuppance • A
weekend lovelier than anything in the world*

Weeks had gone by since the twins first changed places, weeks
when every minute, every little incident, every encounter
threatened danger and discovery. Weeks with a good deal of
heartache and many General Delivery letters demanding
urgent and additional information.

But everything turned out for the best. Partly, of course, by
good luck. Lisa had "again" become an expert cook. The
teachers in Munich had become more or less used to the fact
that the little Horn girl had come back from her vacation less
industrious, less tidy and attentive but, on the other hand,
more lively and quick on the uptake.

And the teachers in Vienna were quite pleased to find that
Conductor Palfy's daughter worked harder in class and was
much better at arithmetic. Only yesterday in the teachers'
room, Miss Gestettner had remarked rather pompously to Miss
Bruckbaur, "It is a most instructive experience, my dear

Miss Bruckbaur, for anyone in pedagogy to follow the development of Lisa Palfy—to see an excess of temperament changing into quiet, controlled, and effective strength and high spirits, fun and a fitful desire for knowledge into a constant and conscientious effort toward education. Well, my dear Miss Bruckbaur, one might almost call it unique. And don't forget that this transformation, this metamorphosis of a character into something higher and more disciplined, has arisen from the child's inner resources, without any educative pressure from without."

Miss Bruckbaur nodded momentously and answered, "This unfolding of character, this individual will to achieve form, is apparent also in the changes in Lisa's handwriting. I always say the handwriting and character . . ."

Peterkin, Dr. Strobel's dog, for some time had resumed his old habit of saying how-do-you-do to the little girl at Conductor Palfy's table. He had resigned himself to the fact, although it was beyond his canine comprehension, that Lisa no longer smelled like Lisa. Human beings are capable of *so* many things, why not of that, too? Besides, she did not eat as many stuffed pancakes as before and seemed to have developed a healthy appetite for meat. When you consider that pancakes have no bones, while chops can be safely counted on to contain them, you can easily understand how Dr. Strobel's dog had overcome his initial reserve.

If Lisa's teachers found a surprising change in Lisa, what would they have thought, supposing they had known her, of

Rosa the housekeeper? For Rosa—of that there can be no doubt—had become quite a different person. Perhaps she was not at heart deceitful and idle and slatternly. Perhaps she was like that only because no one had expected anything else of her.

Since Lottie had been there, gently but firmly checking up and finding out all there was to know about the household, Rosa had developed into a model housekeeper.

Lottie had persuaded her father to hand over the housekeeping money to her instead of giving it to Rosa. And it was quite comic to see Rosa knock at Lottie's door, and go in and ask a nine-year-old girl, who was sitting gravely at her desk doing her homework, for some housekeeping money. Rosa reported faithfully what she wanted to buy, what she would cook for supper, and the other necessary household details.

Lottie would quickly add up the cost, take the money out of her desk, hand it over to Rosa, write down the amount in a notebook, and then, in the evening, there was a general settlement of accounts over the kitchen table.

Even her father had noticed that less money was spent on the housekeeping; that, although the household cost him less, there were always fresh flowers on the table (not only at home but in his studio on Ring Street too!) and that altogether things were much more homelike in Rotenturm Street. ("Just as if there were a woman in the house," he thought to himself, and the idea startled him quite a bit.)

Miss Irene Gerlach, the praline-lady, had noticed that Mr.

Palfy spent more and more time at home. And, in a way, she challenged him about it. Very carefully, for musicians are sensitive people.

"Do you know," he said to her, "when I came in the other day, Lisa was sitting at the piano strumming away happily at the keys. And she was singing a little song, too. Quite sweet! And yet in the old days she wouldn't have gone near a piano if you had tried to drag her there with a tractor."

"And?" asked Miss Gerlach. And her eyebrows went up till they nearly met her hair.

"And?" Mr. Palfy gave an embarrassed laugh. "Since then I've been giving her piano lessons. She finds it great fun. So do I."

Miss Gerlach looked quite scornful. For she was an intellectual. Then she said pointedly, "I thought you were a composer, not a piano teacher for little girls."

No one would have dared in the old days to say that to Mr. Palfy's face. But he laughed like a schoolboy. "But I've never composed so much in my life as I'm doing now," he cried, "or such good stuff!"

"What is it going to be?" she asked.

"A children's opera," he answered.

Her teachers thought Lisa had changed, Lottie knew that Rosa and Peterkin had changed, and her father began to see that the apartment in Rotenturm Street had changed. What a lot of changes!

And in Munich there had been all kinds of changes, too. When her mother noticed that Lottie was no longer so domestic at home or so hard-working at school, but seemed to have become more unpredictable and high-spirited, she went into consultation with herself and this is the kind of thing she thought:

Now, Lisalottie, you had a tractable little child and, instead of letting her be a child, you made her into a housekeeper. Then she spent a few short weeks with children of her own age by a lake in the mountains and

*became what she ought to have been all along—a happy
little girl, hardly worried at all about your troubles.
You've been much too selfish. Shame on you! You ought
to be delighted that Lottie is happy and carefree. What
if she does smash a plate once in a while? What if she does
bring home a letter from her teacher saying that in recent
weeks she has become much less attentive, less tidy and
industrious, and that only yesterday she gave her schoolmate Annie Habersetzer, on four separate occasions, a
good hard slap? No matter what trouble a mother has,
her first duty is to guard her child from being driven too
soon out of the paradise of childhood.*

Thus Mrs. Horn spoke seriously to herself, and said much
more in the same vein. And at last, one day, she spoke to Miss
Linnekogel, her daughter's teacher. "I want Lottie," she said,
"to be a child and not a stunted little grownup! I would rather
have her a happy, genuine little girl than be forced at all
costs to be your best pupil.

"But Lottie used to manage to combine both qualities,"
returned Miss Linnekogel, slightly piqued.

"Why she cannot do so any longer, I do not know," replied
Mrs. Horn. "As a woman who has to earn her own living, I
don't know enough about my daughter. The change must be
connected in some way with her summer vacation. But I know
one thing—she can no longer be what she used to be. And
that is all that matters."

Miss Linnekogel grasped energetically at her spectacles. "I, as your daughter's teacher and guide, must have other aims in view for her. I must and shall attempt to restore your child's inner harmony."

"Do you really think that a bit of inattention in the arithmetic lesson and a few blots in her writing exercises . . ."

"A good example, Mrs. Horn! Her writing exercises! Lottie's writing shows clearly how much she has lost her—how shall I put it—her spiritual balance. But let us leave the question of her writing. Do you think it right that Lottie should take to hitting the other girls?"

"Girls!" Mrs. Horn intentionally emphasized the plural. "As far as I know she has hit no one but Annie Habersetzer."

"Isn't that enough?"

"And this Annie Habersetzer thoroughly deserved it. She had it coming to her."

"But Mrs. Horn!"

"A big, greedy girl who vents her spite on the smallest child in the class—I should not expect her teacher to defend her!"

"What is this story? I had no idea!"

"Then ask poor little Elsa Merck. Perhaps she can tell you something about it."

"But why didn't Lottie tell me when I punished her?"

Then Mrs. Horn drew herself up a little and answered, "Perhaps she hadn't—how did you put it—enough spiritual balance." Then she dashed off to the office. She had to take a taxi to get there in time. Two marks and thirty pfennigs. Oh, dear, what a waste of money!

At noon on Saturday, Mommy suddenly packed a knapsack. "Put on your walking shoes," she said. "We're going to Garmisch, and we won't be back till tomorrow night."

Her daughter asked rather anxiously, "Mommy, can we afford it?"

Mrs. Horn felt a little pang. Then she laughed. "If we spend all our money, I shall have to sell you."

Her daughter danced with glee. "Fine! And when you have the money, I'll give my purchasers the slip. And when you've sold me three or four times, we'll have so much that you won't need to work for a month."

"Do you cost as much as that?"

"Three thousand marks and eleven pfennigs! And I'm going to take my mouth organ with me."

What a weekend it was! Like raspberries and whipped cream! From Garmisch they tramped through the forest, passing a lovely lake, and on to Lake Eib, playing the mouth organ and singing songs. Then down through tall woods they went, slipping and stumbling. On Saturday evening they reached a village, where they took a room with one big bed. And when they had eaten an immense supper from their knapsack, they slept together in the one bed. Outside in the fields the grasshoppers sang a thin serenade. . . . On Sunday morning they went on their way.

A great, snow-capped mountain shone white as silver. Men and women in peasant costume were coming out of church. Cows stood around in the village street as though gossiping over their morning coffee.

And then on again. That was a tough bit of walking. Near some grazing horses, amidst millions of meadow flowers, they ate boiled eggs and cheese sandwiches, and followed them up with a short afternoon nap in the grass. Later they dropped down between wild raspberry bushes and dancing butterflies, back toward Lake Eib. Cowbells tinkled all around them. They saw, crawling along the sky, the cable railway to the snow-capped peak. The lake looked tiny in the bowl of the valley.

"As though God had thrown down a two-mark piece," said Lisa, thoughtfully.

Of course they swam in Lake Eib. And Mommy bought them coffee and cakes on the hotel terrace. And then it was time to take the road back to Garmisch.

Sunburned and happy they sat in the train. And the nice gentleman opposite obstinately refused to believe that the girl sitting next to Lisa was really her mother and had to earn her own living.

At home they dropped into their beds like sacks of potatoes. The last thing Lisa said was, "Mommy, today was lovely! Lovelier than anything in the world!"

Her mother lay awake for a while. How often in the past she had deprived her daughter of pleasures she might easily have had! Well, it was not too late. She could still make up for it.

Then Mrs. Horn fell asleep also. A smile dreamed on her face and flitted across her cheeks like the wind over Lake Eib.

Her daughter had changed. And now the young mother was beginning to change too.

*Mr. Gabel's windows are too small • Afternoon
coffee at Ring Street • Fathers must know when
to be firm • Marriage plans • 43 Kollmann
Avenue • Miss Gerlach is all ears • Mr. Palfy pets a doll.*

Lottie's talent for the piano was lying idle. It was not her
fault. But lately her father had not had much time for giving
lessons. Perhaps that was because of his work on the children's
opera.

Girls have a way of knowing when something is wrong.
When fathers talk of children's operas and never speak of
stylish young ladies, their daughters know which way the wind
is blowing.

Lottie came out of their Rotenturm Street apartment door
and rang the bell next door. A painter named Gabel lived
there, a nice, friendly man who had said he would like to make
a drawing of his neighbor when she could spare the time, Mr.
Gabel opened the door. "Oh, it's Lisa!"

"I have time today," she said.

He invited Lottie in, sat her in an armchair, took up a pad, and began to sketch. "You don't play the piano these days," he remarked.

"Did it disturb you very much?"

"Not a bit. On the contrary, I miss it."

"Daddy hasn't much time now," she said solemnly. "He's composing an opera. A children's opera."

Mr. Gabel was glad to hear it. Then he began to get irritable. "These windows," he grumbled. "You can't see a thing. I ought to have a real studio."

"Then why don't you get one, Mr. Gabel?"

"Because there are none to be found. Studios are very scarce."

The little girl said after a pause, "Daddy has a studio. With big windows. And a skylight."

Mr. Gabel grunted.

"On Ring Street," added Lottie. And after another pause, "You don't need as much light for composing music as you do for painting, do you?"

"No," said Mr. Gabel.

Lottie groped her way a step further. She said thoughtfully, "Daddy could even change with you. Then you would have bigger windows and more light for painting. And Daddy would have a place for composing right next to our own apartment!" The idea seemed to please her immensely. "Wouldn't that be very practical?"

Mr. Gabel could have made all kinds of objections to Lottie's idea. But she would not have understood. So he said with

a smile, "Yes, it would be very practical. The only question is whether your Daddy would think so."

Lottie nodded. "As soon as he gets back, I'll ask him."

Mr. Palfy was sitting in his studio. He had a visitor. A lady visitor. Miss Irene Gerlach had "happened" to have some shopping to do in the neighborhood, and so she had thought to herself, "I'll just drop in and see Arnold. Why not?"

So Arnold had put aside the pages of the score on which he had been working and was chatting with Irene. At first he was a little angry, for he could not for the life of him stand people dropping in and interrupting his work without first making an appointment. But gradually he yielded to the pleasure of sitting with this charming lady.

Irene Gerlach knew what she wanted. She wanted to marry Mr. Palfy. He was famous. She liked him. He liked her. So there were no insurmountable difficulties in the way. It is true that he knew nothing as yet about his future happiness. But she would tactfully let him know in good time. And he would end up by imagining that the idea of marriage had come to him quite spontaneously.

But there was *one* obstacle—that stupid child. But when Irene had presented Arnold with a baby or two, that would come right all by itself. Irene Gerlach would find a way to handle that shy, serious little girl!

The bell rang.

Arnold opened the door.

And who stood in the doorway? The shy, serious little girl. She had a bunch of flowers in her hand, and she said, "Hello, Daddy. I've brought you some fresh flowers." Then she walked into the studio, nodded to the visitor, picked up a vase, and disappeared into the kitchen.

Irene smiled maliciously. "When I see you with your daughter, I have the impression that she keeps you under her thumb."

The composer laughed awkwardly. "She's been acting lately in a very determined way, and what she does is absolutely right—so what can I do?"

As Miss Gerlach shrugged her pretty shoulders Lottie appeared on the scene again. First she put the fresh flowers on the table. Then she brought out cups and saucers and said to her father, as she put them on the table, "I'm making some coffee. We must offer your guest some refreshment."

Daddy and his guest looked after her, perplexed. "And I thought the child was shy!" Miss Gerlach reflected. "Heavens, what a fool I was!"

In a few minutes Lottie reappeared with coffee, sugar, and cream. She poured out the coffee—quite the housewife—asked if Miss Gerlach took sugar, handed her the cream, and sat down beside her father. Then she said with a friendly smile, "I'll just have a cup to keep you company."

Mr. Palfy poured her out a cup of coffee and asked politely, "How much cream, madam?"

Lottie giggled. "Half and half, if you please, sir."

"There you are, madam."

"Thank you very much, sir."

They drank the coffee. They sat in silence. At last Lottie opened the conversation. "I've just been to see Mr. Gabel."

"Has he been drawing a picture of you?" asked her father.

"He started one," she said. Another sip of coffee, then she added innocently, "He hasn't enough light. What he needs most of all is a skylight. Like you have here. . . ."

"Then he should get a studio with a skylight," remarked the conductor, very decidedly but without a suspicion that he was moving in the precise direction that his daughter wanted him to.

"I told him that," she explained calmly. "But all the studios are rented."

"The little beast!" thought Miss Gerlach, who saw just what the child was aiming at. Here it came:

"You don't really need a skylight for composing, Daddy, do you?"

"No, not really."

Lottie took a deep breath, looked down hard at her lap, and said, as though the question had just occurred to her, "Suppose you were to swap with Mr. Gabel, Daddy?" Thank goodness, she had got it out at last! Lottie squinted up sideways at her father. Her eyes were full of timid entreaty.

Half irritated, half amused, he glanced from the little girl to the young lady, who had just time to conjure up a gently ironic smile.

"Then Mr. Gabel would have his studio," said the child, and her voice shook a little, "with all the light he needs. And you would work next to the flat. Next to Rosa and me." Lottie's eyes went down on their knees before her father's. "You would be just as much alone as you are here, Daddy. And when you don't want to be alone, you can come across the hall and be with us. You won't even need to put your hat on. And we can have lunch at home. When lunch is ready, we'll ring your bell three times. We'll always have your favorite dishes— even smoked ham. And when you play the piano, we'll be able to hear it through the wall . . ." The childish voice had grown more and more uncertain. Now it stopped.

Miss Gerlach suddenly rose from her chair. She had to rush home. How the time had passed! But the conversation had been just too terribly interesting!

Mr. Palfy went to the door with her. He kissed her perfumed hand. "Till tonight," he said.

"Perhaps you will be otherwise engaged?"

"What do you mean?"

She smiled. "Perhaps you will be moving!"

He laughed.

"Don't laugh too soon! From what I know of your daughter, she has probably already made arrangements with the furniture movers." The lady swept furiously down the stairs.

When Mr. Palfy came back into the studio, Lottie was already washing the coffee cups. He played a few notes on the piano. He strode up and down the room. He stared at the notes he had scribbled on the score.

Lottie took great care not to make a noise with the cups and saucers. When she had wiped them dry and put them back in the cupboard, she put on her hat and went quietly into the studio.

"Good-by, Daddy . . ."

"Good-by."

"Are you coming home to supper?"

"No. Not today."

The little girl slowly nodded and timidly held out her hand.

"Listen, Lisa, I don't like other people interfering with my affairs, not even my own daughter! I know myself what's good for me."

"Of course, Daddy," she said calmly and gently. She was still holding out her hand.

At last he took it and, as he did so, he saw that there were tears on her eyelashes.

A father must know when to be firm. So he pretended not to notice anything unusual, nodded shortly, and sat down at his grand piano.

Lottie went softly to the door, softly opened it, and left.

Mr. Palfy ran his fingers through his hair. Tears! Another distraction to cope with! And he was trying to compose a children's opera. He could hardly endure seeing a little thing like that with tears in her eyes. They hung on her long lashes like dewdrops on tiny blades of grass.

His hands struck a few notes. He bent his head and listened. He played the phrase again. He repeated it in another key. It was the minor variation of a gay song he had written for his opera. He altered the rhythm. And went on working.

More weeks passed. Miss Irene Gerlach did not forget the little scene in the studio. And, as for Lottie's proposal that her father should exchange his place on Ring Street for Mr. Gabel's apartment, she understood it for what it was: a challenge to battle! She was quick to accept the challenge. She knew her weapons. She knew how to use them. She knew how effective they were. She shot all her arrows into that quivering target, the artistic heart of Mr. Palfy. Every shot was a bull's-eye. He was quite helpless.

"I want you to be my wife," he said, and it sounded like a command.

She stroked his hair and said with a little mocking smile, "Then tomorrow I'll put on my best frock, darling, and go and ask your daughter's consent."

Another arrow was sticking in his heart. And this time it was a poisoned one.

Mr. Gabel was sketching Lottie. Suddenly he lowered his pad and pencil and said, "What's wrong with you today, Lisa? You look like a rainy weekend!"

The little girl took a long breath, as though she had a heap of stones on her chest. "Oh, it's nothing much."

"Anything to do with school?"

She shook her head. "That wouldn't worry me."

Mr. Gabel laid down his pad. "Do you know what we'll do, you little misery? We'll stop working for today." He stood up. "Let's go for a walk. That will help to take your mind off it."

"I think I'll play the piano a bit."

"Better still," he said. "I'll hear you through the wall. So I'll get something out of it, too."

She shook his hand, curtsied, and went out.

He looked thoughtfully after her. He knew how heavily trouble can weigh on a child's heart. He had been a child himself once and, unlike a good many people, had not forgotten it.

When the strum of a piano came from the next apartment, he nodded approvingly and began to whistle the tune.

Then he took up his brush and palette, studied his work with screwed-up eyes, and got on with the job.

Mr. Arnold Palfy arrived home at his apartment in Rotenturm Street. The stairs seemed twice as long as usual. He hung his hat and coat in the closet. So Lisa was playing the piano? Well, she would have to stop and listen to him for a bit. He straightened his jacket as though he were about to pay a call on the director of the opera. Then he opened the door of the sitting room.

The little girl looked up from the keys and smiled at him. "Daddy! How lovely!" She jumped down from the piano stool.

"Shall I make you some coffee?" She turned to go to the kitchen.

He caught her arm. "No, thank you," he said. "I want to talk to you. Sit down!"

She sat down in a huge winged chair, where she looked no bigger than a doll, smoothed out her plaid skirt, and looked up at him expectantly.

He cleared his throat nervously, took a few steps up and

down, and finally stopped by the wing chair. "Well, Lisa," he began, "I want to talk to you about a serious and important matter. I have been alone since your mother—er—since your mother has not been here. That's over seven years. Of course not entirely alone, for I've had you. And I have you still."

The child looked up at him, wide-eyed.

"What nonsense I'm talking," he thought. He was rather annoyed with himself. "The main point is," he went on, "I don't wish to be alone any longer. There's going to be a change. In my life and therefore in yours, too."

The room was very still.

A fly buzzed loudly as it tried to butt its way through the windowpane into the fresh air outside. It was a pure waste of time and could only result in damage to its insect head.

"I have decided to marry again."

"No!" said the little girl clearly. It sounded like a cry of pain. Then she repeated softly, "No, please, Daddy! No, please! Please, please, no!"

"You know Miss Gerlach. She's very fond of you. And she'll make you a good mother. It wouldn't be right for you to go on growing up in a household without any womanly influence."

Lottie went on shaking her head and moving her lips without saying anything. Like an automaton that cannot stop working. It was frightening to see.

So her father glanced quickly away again, and said, "You will get used to the new situation faster than you think. Cruel stepmothers only happen in fairy tales. So I know I can rely on you, Lisa. You are the most sensible little person I've ever come across." He looked at the clock. "There! Now I must go. I've got to rehearse *Rigoletto* with Mr. Luser." And he was gone.

The little girl sat there stupefied.

Mr. Palfy reached the hall and put his hat back on his head. Then there was a cry from the living room. "Daddy!" It sounded as though someone were drowning.

"People don't drown in living rooms," thought Mr. Palfy as he slipped out. He was in a great hurry. For, of course, he had to rehearse with Mr. Luser.

Lottie finally awakened from her stupor. Even in her despair her common sense did not desert her. What was she to do? For unquestionably she had to do something. Daddy could never marry another woman, never! He already had a wife. Even if she was not living with him. Never would Lottie accept a new mother, never! She *had* a mother, her Mommy, whom she loved more than anyone else in the world!

Perhaps Mommy could help. But Lottie could not tell her. She could not let her know the two children's big secret, and least of all the fact that her father wanted to marry this Miss Gerlach.

So there was only one way left, and Lottie had to go that way herself, without help.

She got the telephone directory. She turned the pages with trembling fingers. "Gerlach." There were not very many Gerlachs. Finally—*Gerlach, Stefan. Managing Director, Vienna Hotel Company, 43 Kollmann Avenue.* (Daddy had mentioned recently that Miss Gerlach's father owned a number of restaurants and hotels, including the Imperial, where they went every day to luncheon.)

When Rosa had explained how to get to Kollmann Avenue, Lottie put on her hat and coat. "I'm going out now," she said.

"What are you going to Kollmann Avenue for?" asked Rosa curiously.

"I want to speak to someone."

"Well, don't be long."

Lottie nodded and set out.

A parlormaid entered Irene Gerlach's charming room and smiled. "There's a child to see you, madam. A little girl."

Madam had just done her fingernails and was waving her hands in the air to help dry the polish. "A little girl?"

"Her name is Lisa Palfy."

"Oh," said madam, with a slight drawl. "Show her in!"

The parlormaid withdrew. The young lady rose, glanced at herself in the mirror, and could not help smiling at her own tense and earnest expression.

As Lottie entered the room, Miss Gerlach said to the parlormaid, "Make us some chocolate and bring some éclairs." Then she turned graciously to her visitor. "How sweet of you to come and see me. It shows how thoughtless I am. I ought to have invited you long ago. Won't you take your coat off?"

"No, thank you," said Lottie. "I won't stay long."

"Oh?" Irene Gerlach lost nothing of her patronizing manner. "But you'll have time to sit down?" Lottie perched herself on the edge of a chair, never taking her eyes off the lady.

Irene Gerlach began to find the situation awkward and ridiculous. But she controlled herself. After all, there was something at stake. Something she was anxious to win, something she was determined to win. "I suppose you just happened to be down this way?"

"No. I have something to say to you."

Irene Gerlach smiled enchantingly. "I am all ears. What is it?"

Lottie got off the chair, stood in the middle of the room, and said slowly, "Daddy said you wanted to marry him."

"Did he really say that?" Miss Gerlach's laugh was clear as a bell. "Didn't he really say that he wants to marry me? Still, that doesn't really matter. It's quite true, Lisa. Your father and I want to marry each other. And you and I are going to get on well together. I'm sure of it. Aren't you? Listen, when we have lived together for a little while, we'll be the best of friends. We'll both do all we can, won't we? Shake hands on it."

Lottie stepped back and said emphatically, "You mustn't marry Daddy."

This was certainly going too far. "And why not?"

"Because you mustn't."

"Not a very good reason," said the young lady sharply. She

was getting nowhere with kindness. "Are you trying to forbid me to marry your father?"

"Yes!"

"Well, I've never heard such nonsense!" She was becoming angry. "I must ask you to go home now. I don't know whether I shall tell your father of this curious visit. I'll think it over. But if I don't tell him, it will be because I don't want to put serious obstacles in the way of our future friendship. For I still want to believe that we shall be friends. *Auf Wiedersehen!*"

Lottie turned again at the door, and said, "Leave us alone! Please, please . . ." Then she was gone.

Miss Gerlach decided there was only one thing to do—hasten the preparations for the marriage. And when that was over, she must arrange to pack the child off to a boarding school. Without delay. Nothing would help but strict discipline at the hands of strangers.

"What do *you* want?"

The parlormaid was there with a tray. "I've brought the chocolate. And the éclairs. What's become of the little girl?"

"Get out!"

Mr. Palfy did not come home to dinner, for he was conducting at the Opera House. Rosa kept Lottie company, as she always did in her father's absence.

"You're not eating a thing," remarked Rosa reproachfully. "And you look like a ghost. What's the matter?"

Lottie shook her head and said nothing. The housekeeper took her hand and quickly dropped it again. "You're feverish! Off to bed with you!" Then, grunting and panting, she carried the unprotesting child to her room, undressed her, and put her to bed.

"Don't tell Daddy!" whispered Lottie. Her teeth were chattering. Rosa piled up blankets and pillows. Then she ran to the telephone and called Dr. Strobel.

The old gentleman promised to come at once. He was as worried as Rosa.

She telephoned to the Opera House. "All right," someone answered. "We'll tell Mr. Palfy during the intermission."

Rosa flew back to the bedroom. Lottie was tossing about in the bed, stammering confused, meaningless words. The pillows and blankets were on the floor.

If only Dr. Strobel would come! What should she do? Compresses? But what sort? Hot? Cold? Wet? Dry?

Conductor Palfy, in white tie and tails, was spending the intermission in the soprano's dressing room. They talked shop. Theater people have only one topic of conversation—the theater. That cannot be helped. There was a knock at the door. "Come in!"

The stage manager entered. "So here you are at last, Mr. Palfy!" cried the fidgety old man. "We've had a call from your home in Rotenturm Street. Your daughter has been taken suddenly ill. Dr. Strobel was called immediately and by this time he ought to be with her." The conductor turned very pale.

"Thank you, Hermann," he said in a low voice. The stage manager withdrew.

"I hope it's nothing serious," said the soprano. "Has she had measles?"

"No," he said and got up. "Excuse me." As the door closed behind him, he broke into a run.

He was telephoning. "Hello, Irene!"

"Yes, darling? Is the performance over so soon? I'm not half ready to come out."

He told her hurriedly what he had just heard. Then he said,

"I'm afraid I shan't be able to take you out tonight."

"Of course not. I hope it's nothing serious. Has she had measles?"

"No," he answered impatiently. "I'll ring you again to-morrow morning." Then he put down the receiver.

A gong sounded. The intermission was over. Life and the opera went on.

At last the opera was over. The conductor was racing up the stairs in Rotenturm Street. Rosa admitted him. She still had on her hat, for she had just been out to the drugstore.

Dr. Strobel was sitting beside the bed.

"How is she?" asked her father in a whisper.

"Not at all well," answered the doctor. "But you needn't whisper. I've given her an injection."

Lottie lay on the pillows, flushed and fighting for breath. Her face was contorted with pain, as though she were tormented by the artificial sleep which the old doctor had imposed on her.

"Measles?"

"Not a trace."

Rosa entered the room, snuffling back her tears.

"For goodness sake, take your hat off!" cried the conductor irritably.

"Oh, dear! Excuse me!" She removed her hat and held it in her hand.

Dr. Strobel looked inquiringly at the two of them.

"She is evidently going through a severe mental crisis," he said. "Do you know anything about it? No? Well, can you make any guesses?"

Rosa said, "I don't know whether this has anything to do with it, but—she went out this afternoon. She said she had to speak to someone. And before she went, she asked me the way to Kollmann Avenue."

"Kollmann Avenue?" repeated the doctor and looked across at Mr. Palfy.

Mr. Palfy went quickly into the next room and telephoned. "Did Lisa come to see you this afternoon?"

"Yes," said a feminine voice. "But how did she happen to tell you?"

He made no reply to that, but went on. "What did she want?"

Miss Gerlach laughed. "You had better ask her yourself."

"Answer me, please!" It was lucky she could not see his face.

"If you want to know, she came to forbid me to marry you," she returned sharply.

He mumbled something and hung up. "What's the matter with her?" asked Miss Gerlach. Then she became aware that she had been cut off. "The little beast!" she exclaimed, half aloud. "She stops at nothing! Going off to bed and pretending to be ill!"

The doctor prepared to leave. Mr. Palfy stopped him at the door. "What's wrong with the child?"

"A nervous fever. I'll look in first thing tomorrow morning. Good night."

The conductor went into Lottie's room, sat down by the bed, and said to Rosa, "I won't need you any more. Good night."

"But hadn't I better . . ."

He looked at her.

She went. She still had her hat in her hand.

He stroked the hot little cheek. Lottie started in her feverish sleep and writhed away from him.

He looked around the room. Her schoolbag lay ready on the seat by the desk. And beside it lay Christel, her doll.

He got up stealthily, picked up Christel, put out the light, and sat down by the bed again.

He sat in the dark, stroking the doll as though it were a child. A child that did not move away from the touch of his hand.

Mr. Appeldauer's photographs produce
complications • Is it Lottie? • Charred pork chops and
broken plates • Why no word from Lottie?

Mr. Bernau, editor of the *Munich Illustrated,* groaned aloud.
"The silly season, my dear! Where can we get a front-page
news picture without stealing it?"

Mrs. Horn, standing beside his desk, remarked, "Neo-Press
has sent some photos of the new women's breast-stroke cham-
pion."

"Is she pretty?"

The young woman smiled. "Passable."

Mr. Bernau waved the idea aside with an air of discourage-
ment. Then he began to ransack his desk.

"A comic village photographer sent me in some pictures
weeks ago. Photos of twins." He searched among folders and
copies of old newspapers. "Two enchanting little girls! Alike
as two peas! Come on, what's become of you, you little minxes?
That sort of thing always goes big. All it needs is a snappy caption. In the absence of real news pictures, what's wrong with

a pair of charming twins? Ah, here you are!" He had found
the envelope. He studied the photographs and nodded approvingly. "We'll use one of these, Mrs. Horn." He handed her
the photographs.

Presently he looked up, for his picture editor had not said
a word. "Hey!" he cried. "What's the matter? Why, you're like
Lot's wife—a pillar of salt. Wake up! Do you feel ill, Mrs.
Horn?"

"Not too well, Mr. Bernau." Her voice shook. She stared
at the photograph. She read the name of the sender—*Joseph
Appeldauer, Photographer, Bohrlaken on Lake Bohren.*

Everything was going around and around in her head.

"Pick out the best picture and write me a caption that'll
make our readers' hearts sing for joy. It's just your style."

"I wonder if we ought to publish them," she heard herself say.

"Why not?"

"I don't believe they are genuine."

"You think it's a fake?" Mr. Bernau laughed. "You overrate the good Mr. Appeldauer. He's not as clever as all that. Well, to work, my dear! You can leave the caption till the morning, if you like. Let me see it before it goes into print." He nodded and bent over the next item.

She groped her way back to her office, dropped into her chair, put down the photographs in front of her, and pressed her hands to her brow.

Her thoughts whirled around in her head. The twins! Bohrlaken! The summer camp! Of course! But why had Lottie never said anything about it? Why hadn't Lottie brought the photographs back with her? For when the twins had their pictures taken, they must have meant to bring them home! Then, of course, they found out that they were sisters. And then decided to say nothing about it. It was understandable—yes, indeed it was. Heavens, how alike they were! Not even the proverbial mother's eye could tell the difference! Oh, my darlings! My two darlings!

If Mr. Bernau had put his head around the door at that moment, he would have seen a face overwhelmed with joy and pain; tears streaming down, tears that drain the heart, as though life itself were pouring from the eyes.

Luckily, Mr. Bernau did not put his head around the door.

Mrs. Horn did her best to pull herself together. She *must* keep her head! What was going to happen? What did she want to happen? She decided to speak to Lottie.

An ice-cold thought went through her. A thought that shook her like an invisible hand.

The girl she would speak to—*was* she Lottie?

Mrs. Horn sought out her daughter's teacher, Miss Linnekogel, in her home.

"The question you have asked me," said Miss Linnekogel, "is an exceedingly strange one. Do I think it possible that your daughter is not your daughter but another girl? Excuse me, but . . ."

"No, I'm not mad," Mrs. Horn assured her, and laid a photograph on the table.

Miss Linnekogel looked at it. Then at her visitor. Then at the photograph again.

"I have two daughters," said Mrs. Horn in a low voice. "The second lives with my divorced husband in Vienna. This photograph happened to come into my hands a few hours ago. I did not know that the two children had met during camp."

Miss Linnekogel opened and closed her mouth like a gasping fish. She shook her head and pushed the photograph away as though she were afraid it would bite her. At last she asked, "Didn't they know of each other's existence before that meeting?"

Mrs. Horn shook her head. "No. My husband and I agreed when we parted that they should be kept in ignorance. We thought it was the best way."

"And you, yourself, never heard again from your husband or your other daughter?"

"Never."

"Do you think he has remarried?"

"I don't know. I doubt it. He thought he was unsuited for family life."

"A most astonishing story," said the teacher. "Could the children really have hit on the fantastic idea of changing places? When you consider the change in Lottie's character— and her writing, Mrs. Horn, her writing! It seems hardly believable, and yet it would certainly provide an explanation for several things."

Mrs. Horn nodded and looked straight in front of her.

"Forgive my frankness," went on Miss Linnekogel. "I have never been married. I have no children. I am a teacher—but I always think that women, I mean married women, attach too much importance to their husbands. Nothing is really important except the happiness of the children."

Mrs. Horn smiled wryly. "Do you believe that my children would have been happier if my husband and I had lived together unhappily?"

Miss Linnekogel said thoughtfully, "I'm not reproaching you. You are still very young. You were hardly more than a child when you married. All your life you will be younger than I have ever been. What is right for one may be wrong for another."

Her visitor stood up.

"And what will you do?"

"If I only knew!" said Mrs. Horn.

Lisa was standing at the widow of a Munich post office. "No," said the clerk in charge of General Delivery, and his voice was sympathetic. "No, Miss Forget-me-not, nothing for you again."

Lisa looked at him doubtfully. "What can it mean?" she said miserably.

The clerk tried a little joke. "Perhaps the not's fallen off the forget-me-not."

"No fear of that!" she said, as though to herself. "I'll come again tomorrow."

"We'll do our best for you," he said, smiling.

When Mrs. Horn reached home, her heart was a battleground of hot curiosity and cold fear; she could hardly get her breath.

Her daughter was busy in the kitchen. There was a clatter of saucepan lids. Something was simmering on the stove.

"It smells good," said Mrs. Horn. "What's for dinner?"

"Pork chops with sauerkraut and scalloped potatoes," returned her daughter proudly.

"How quickly you've learned to cook!" said Mrs. Horn with seeming innocence.

"Yes, haven't I?" answered her daughter gaily. "I never thought I—" She broke off in alarm and bit her lip. At all costs she must avoid meeting her mother's eye.

Mrs. Horn leaned against the doorframe. She was white, white as the wall behind her.

The little girl was at the open cupboard door, taking out the plates, which clattered together as though there were an earthquake.

Her mother opened her mouth with an effort. "Lisa!" she said.

Crash!

The plates were in fragments on the floor. Lisa had spun around. Her eyes were wide with fright.

"Lisa!" repeated her mother gently, and held out her arms.

"Mommy!"

The little girl hung on her mother's neck as though she were drowning. She sobbed passionately.

Her mother stroked the child with trembling hands. "My child, my darling child!"

They knelt there among the smashed plates. The pork chops were burning on the stove. There was a smell of charred meat. Water spat and hissed from the saucepans onto the gas jets.

The woman and the little girl were unaware—they were, as is often said, though seldom truthfully, "in another world."

Some hours had passed. Lisa had confessed and Mommy had forgiven her. It had been a long, complicated confession, followed by a brief, unspoken absolution for all the sins committed—a look, a kiss—nothing more was needed.

Now they were sitting on the sofa. Lisa had snuggled close, very close, to her mother. Oh, how wonderful it was to have told the truth at last! How free she felt, as free as air! She had to cling tightly to her mother for fear she might suddenly float away.

"What a clever pair you are!"

Lisa giggled with pride. There was *one* secret she had not yet revealed—the existence in Vienna of a certain Miss Gerlach, about whom Lottie had written some anxious letters.

Her mother sighed.

Lisa looked up apprehensively.

"Well, my dear," said her mother, "I'm wondering what's next? Can we go on acting as though nothing had happened?"

Lisa shook her head firmly. "Lottie must be simply longing for you. And you for her too, aren't you, Mommy?"

Her mother nodded.

"And I am too," confessed Lisa. "For Lottie and . . ."

"And your father?"

Lisa nodded. Eagerly and yet timidly. "I only wish I knew why Lottie hasn't written . . ."

"Yes," murmured her mother. "I'm worried."

*A long-distance call from Munich • Two airplane
tickets to Vienna • Peterkin is struck by
lightning • Conductor Palfy has an unexpected visitor*

Lottie lay listlessly in bed. She was asleep. She was generally asleep. "Weakness," Dr. Strobel had said when he called that morning. Mr. Palfy was sitting beside the bed. For days he had hardly left the room. They had found another conductor for the Opera House. A cot had been brought in so that he could stay constantly with his daughter.

The telephone rang in the next room. Rosa entered the room on tiptoe. "A long-distance call from Munich," she whispered. "Will you take it?"

He got up quietly, making signs to her to stay in the room till he got back. Then he stole silently out to the telephone. Munich? Who could it be? Probably his concert agent, Keller and Company. Why on earth didn't they leave him in peace?

He took up the receiver and gave his name. The exchange put through the call.

"Palfy speaking."

"This is Mrs. Horn," said a woman's voice, all the way from Munich.

"What?" he asked in surprise. "Who? Lisalottie?"

"Yes," said the distant voice. "Please forgive me for telephoning. But I'm worried about the child. I hope she's not ill."

"Yes," he said softly. "She is ill."

"Oh!" The distant voice took on a note of alarm.

Puzzled, Mr. Palfy said, "But I don't understand. How did you . . ."

"We suspected it. Lisa and I."

"Lisa?" He laughed nervously. Then he listened with bewilderment—growing bewilderment. He shook his head. He ran his fingers feverishly through his hair, while the distant voice explained all that could be explained in such breathless haste.

"Are you still speaking?" asked the girl at the switchboard.

"Yes, yes! Don't cut us off!" shouted Mr. Palfy. After all, you can more or less imagine the tumult in the poor man's mind.

"What's the matter with Lottie?" asked the anxious voice of his ex-wife.

"A nervous fever," he answered. "She's passed the crisis, the doctor says. But she's worn out, mentally and physically."

"A good doctor?"

"Certainly—Dr. Strobel. He's known Lisa since she was a baby." He gave a jangled laugh. "Sorry! Of course it's not Lisa, it's Lottie. No, he hasn't known her." He sighed.

And away in Munich a woman sighed also. Two grown-up people completely at a loss. Their hearts and tongues paralyzed. And their brains too, it seemed.

Into that awkward and dangerous silence broke an eager childish voice. "Daddy! Dear, dear Daddy!" The words echoed across the distance. "This is Lisa! Hello, Daddy! Shall we come to Vienna? Shall we come now?"

The saving word had been spoken. The icy constraint of the two grownups melted as at the touch of a spring breeze. "Hello, Lisa!" cried her father longingly. "Yes, that's a good idea!"

"Isn't it, Daddy!" The little girl laughed joyfully.

"When can you get here?"

Then the young woman's voice came again. "I'll find out what time the first train leaves in the morning."

"Take a plane!" he shouted. "You'll get here quicker!" How can I shout like that? he thought. I shall wake her up.

When he got back, Rosa surrendered the place by the side of the bed and began to tiptoe towards the door.

"Rosa," he said softly.

She stopped.

"My wife's coming tomorrow."

"Your wife?"

"Ssh! Not so loud! My ex-wife. Lottie's mother."

"Lottie's?"

He smiled and waved his hand in the air. How was she to

know? "Yes, Lottie. Lisa's coming, too."

"Lisa? What do you mean? There's Lisa." She pointed to the bed.

He shook his head. "No, that's her twin."

"Twin?" The poor woman was hopelessly confused by the family relationships of Conductor Palfy.

"See that there's enough to eat. We'll talk about the sleeping arrangements later."

"Well, bless my soul!" she muttered, as she crept from the room.

Mr. Palfy looked at the exhausted and slumbering child. Her brow glistened with moisture. He took a towel and gently dried her face.

So this was his other little daughter! His Lottie! What courage and strength of mind she had shown before sickness and despair overwhelmed her! She could scarcely have got that courage from her father. From whom, then?

From her mother?

The telephone rang again. Rosa put her head around the door. "Miss Gerlach."

Mr. Palfy shook his head without looking up.

Mrs. Horn was given a leave of absence by Mr. Bernau to attend to "urgent family affairs."

She telephoned the airport and was lucky enough to get two seats on a plane leaving early the following morning. Then she packed the necessities for the trip into a suitcase.

Short as it was, the night seemed endless. But all nights that seem endless do end sometime.

Next morning, as Dr. Strobel, accompanied by Peterkin, arrived outside the house in Rotenturm Street, a taxi drove up. A little girl jumped out of the taxi, and Peterkin sprang at her as though he had suddenly gone mad. He braked, spun around like a top, whimpered with joy, and sprang at her again and again.

"Hello, Peterkin! Hello, Doctor!"

The doctor was too astounded to answer. Suddenly he too sprang at the child—though not as gracefully as Peterkin—and shouted, "Have you gone quite crazy? Get back to bed at once!"

Lisa and Peterkin made a dash for the house. A young lady alighted from the cab.

"That child will catch her death!" cried the doctor, horrified.

"She's not the child you think," said the young lady pleasantly. "She's her sister."

Rosa opened the door of the apartment. She found outside a yapping dog and a little girl.

"Hello, Rosa," said the little girl, and she and Peterkin dashed into Lottie's room.

The housekeeper looked limply after them, and crossed herself.

Then old Dr. Strobel came panting up the stairs. With him came a very pretty young woman who glanced around quickly as she walked by the doctor's side.

"How's Lottie?" asked the woman quickly.

"A little better, I think," said Rosa. "Shall I take you in to see her?"

"I know the way, thank you." And the strange woman also disappeared into Lottie's room.

"When you've recovered a little," said the doctor with a chuckle, "perhaps you'll help me off with my coat. But take your time."

Rosa started. "I beg your pardon, sir," she stammered.

"I don't need to hurry so much today," he explained patiently.

"Mommy!" breathed Lottie. Her eyes, big and shining, hung on her mother's face as though it was a phantom of dream and magic. The young woman silently stroked the hot little hand. She knelt by the bed and took her trembling daughter gently in her arms.

Lisa threw a lightning glance at her father, who was standing by the window. Then she began straightening Lottie's pillows. She beat them, turned them, pulled the sheets smooth. *She* was the little housekeeper now. She had learned it from her mother.

Mr. Palfy stole a sideways glance at the three of them, the mother with her children. *His* children, too, of course. And the young mother had been, years ago, his young wife. Sub-

merged days, forgotten hours, rose up before him. A long, long time ago . . .

Peterkin lay at the foot of the bed as though struck by lightning and kept looking from one little girl to the other. Even the shining black tip of his little nose switched doubtfully towards each child in turn, as though he could not decide what to do next. What a shame to put a nice, affectionate dog into such a quandary!

There was a knock at the door.

The four occupants of the room started as though roused from a strange, waking sleep.

The old doctor came in, jovial and rather noisy as usual. He crossed to the bed. "How's the patient?"

"Fi-i-ine!" breathed Lottie with a worn smile.

"Any sign of an appetite today?" he growled.

"If Mommy cooks," whispered Lottie. Mommy nodded and went over to the window. "Forgive me, Arnold, for not having spoken to you before."

Mr. Palfy shook hands with her. "I'm grateful to you for coming."

"Not at all! What else could I do? The child . . ."

"Of course, the child," he returned. "Still, I'm grateful."

"You look as though you hadn't slept for days," she said uncertainly.

"I shall make up for it. I was anxious about—about the child."

"She'll soon be all right again," said the young woman confidently. "I feel it."

A certain amount of whispering was going on at the bed. Lisa bent close to Lottie's ear. "Mommy doesn't know about Miss Gerlach. We must never tell her, either."

Lottie nodded anxiously.

Old Dr. Strobel could not have heard what they said because he was reading the thermometer. Though, of course, he was not reading it with his ears. And if, after all, he did hear something, no one knew better than he how to avoid showing it.

"The temperature's almost normal," he announced.

"You're over the worst of it. Congratulations, Lisa."

"Thank you, sir," said the real Lisa, giggling.

"Or do you mean me?" asked Lottie, smiling wanly, for her head was still aching.

"You're a pair of conspiring females," he growled. "A fine couple of contriving minxes! You've even led my Peterkin up the garden path."

He put out his two massive hands and gently stroked the girls' heads. Then he gave a tremendous cough and got up. "Come, Peterkin! If you can tear yourself away from those frauds."

Peterkin wagged his tail by way of farewell. Then he snuggled close against the vast trouser leg of the doctor, who was just remarking to Mr. Palfy, "A mother is a kind of medicine you can't buy at the drugstore!" He turned to the young woman. "Can you stay till Lisa—oh, confound it!—till Lottie is quite well again?"

"I think I can. I should like to."

"Then that's settled," said the old gentleman. "Your ex-husband will just have to make the best of it."

Mr. Palfy opened his mouth.

"Don't bother to say it," said the doctor, laughing. "I know what it will do to your artistic temperament having all these people in the apartment! Have patience! You'll soon be nice and lonely again."

He was in fine form today, the old doctor! He opened the

door so suddenly that Rosa, who was listening outside, got a good-sized bump on the head. She put both hands to the buzzing forehead.

"Lay the blade of a cold clean knife on it," he prescribed, every inch the doctor. "That's all right. I'll give you that valuable advice for nothing!"

Night had spread its wings over the earth. In Vienna as everywhere else. There was no sound in the children's room. Lisa was sleeping. Lottie was sleeping too, sleeping herself back to health.

Up to a few minutes ago, Mrs. Horn and Mr. Palfy had been seated in the next room. They had discussed a great many things and had avoided discussing many more. Mr. Palfy finally got up. "Well, I must be off," he said. As he spoke he felt rather foolish. Remember that his own two little girls were sleeping in the next room, and the pretty young woman standing opposite him was their mother, and yet he had to sneak off like a schoolboy who has just had a snub! Sneaking out of his own home! If there are still such things as invisible household spirits—as there used to be in the good old days—how they must have chuckled!

He hesitated. "If she gets worse, you'll find me at the studio."

"You needn't worry," she said confidently. "And don't forget you have a lot of sleep to make up."

He nodded. "Good night."

"Good night."

As he went slowly down the stairs she called softly, "Arnold!" He looked back inquiringly.

"Are you coming back to breakfast?"

"Yes."

When she had locked the door and hooked the chain into place, she stood for a time brooding. He had aged. No doubt of that. He almost looked like a real grown-up man, her ex husband.

Then she looked up and went to keep watch over her sleeping children—hers and his!

An hour later a fashionably dressed young woman alighted from a car outside a house in Ring Street and spoke with an unhelpful attendant.

"Conductor Palfy?" he grunted. "I don't think he's in."

"There's a light in his studio," she pointed out. "So he must be. Here!" She slipped a bill into his hand and hurried past him to the stairs. He stared at the bill and shuffled away.

"You?" said Arnold Palfy, as he opened his door upstairs.

"Right the first time," answered Irene Gerlach sourly and walked into the studio. She sat down, lit a cigarette, and looked at him expectantly.

He said nothing.

"Why did you refuse to speak to me on the telephone?" she asked. "Do you think that was polite?"

"I didn't refuse to speak to you."

"Didn't you?"

"I wasn't capable of speaking. I didn't feel like it. The child was very ill."

"But now she's better. Otherwise you would still be at Rotenturm Street."

He nodded. "Yes, she's better. And my wife is there."

"Who?"

"My wife. My divorced wife. She arrived today with my other child."

"Your *other* child!"

"Yes. They're twins. First Lisa was with me. But since her vacation the other has been here. And yet I didn't even notice it. I found out only yesterday."

The lady laughed angrily. "A little clever planning by your ex-wife!"

"She didn't find out till yesterday, either," he said impatiently.

Irene Gerlach curled her pretty painted lips ironically. "The situation has some piquancy, hasn't it? In one apartment is a woman who is no longer your wife and in the other a woman who is not yet your wife."

His temper rose. "There are many more apartments and, in them, many more women who are not yet my wife."

"Oh! You can be witty too, can you?"

"I'm sorry, Irene. My nerves are on edge."

"I'm sorry, Arnold. So are mine."

Bang! The door was shut and Miss Gerlach was outside it.

Mr. Palfy stared for some time at the closed door. Then he strolled over to the Bösendorfer Grand, looked through the pages of music paper covered with notes for his children's opera, took out one page, and sat down at the keyboard.

For a time he played from his notes. A simple, severe canon in one of the modes of old church music. Then he began to modulate. From the Dorian to C minor, from C minor to E-flat major. And slowly, quite slowly, a new melody bloomed. A tune so simple and winsome that it might have been sung by two little girls with pure, clear, childish voices. In a summer meadow. By a cool mountain lake that mirrored the blue heaven. The heaven that is high above our understanding, where the sun shines, warming all creatures without distinction, whether good, bad, or indifferent.

*Two birthdays but one birthday wish • Cross your
fingers • A crowd at the keyhole*

Lottie was well again, and once more she was wearing her
braids and ribbons. And Lisa had her curls again and could
shake them to her heart's content.

They helped their mother and Rosa with the shopping and
the housework. They played games together. They sang duets
while Lottie—and sometimes even Daddy—played the piano.
They called on Mr. Gabel next door. Or they took Peterkin
for walks, while Dr. Strobel was busy with his patients. Peterkin had adjusted himself to the twofold Lisa, first by doubling
his capacity for loving little girls and then by halving it. He
had to find a solution somehow.

But sometimes the sisters looked anxiously into each other's
eyes. What was going to happen now?

The twins had their birthday celebration. They were sitting
with their parents in the living room. Rosa had made two

cakes, each with ten candles. There had been cups of steaming chocolate. Daddy had played a wonderful "Birthday March for Twins." Now he swung around on the piano stool and said, "Tell me why you wouldn't let us give you any presents."

Lottie took a deep breath and answered, "Because we want something you can't buy."

"What is it you want, darling?" asked Mommy.

Now it was Lisa's turn to take a deep breath. Then she explained, trembling with excitement, "The present Lottie and I want for our birthday is to be able to live together always." It was out at last.

Their parents said nothing.

Lottie added very softly, "Then you needn't ever give us a present again as long as we live! Not for birthdays and not for Christmas. Never at all!"

Mommy and Daddy still said nothing.

"You might try it, anyway." Lisa had tears in her eyes. "We'll be as good as gold—a lot better than we are now. And everything will be a lot, lot better."

Lottie nodded. "We promise!"

"Word of honor and cross our hearts!" added Lisa quickly.

Their father got up from the piano stool. "If you agree, Lisalottie, I think we'll have a word in the next room."

"Yes, Arnold," replied his ex-wife. And then the two of them went into the next room and the door closed behind them.

"Cross your fingers!" whispered Lisa excitedly. Sixteen

small fingers were hastily crossed and four small thumbs clenched tight.

Lottie moved her lips silently.

"Are you saying a prayer?" asked Lisa.

Lottie nodded.

Then Lisa's lips began to move also. "For what we are about to receive may the Lord make us truly thankful," she murmured, half to herself.

Lottie shook her braids reprovingly.

"I know it's out of place," whispered Lisa, a little abashed. "But it's all I can think of. For what we are about to receive may the Lord . . ."

"Putting our own position to one side," Mr. Palfy was just saying in the next room, staring fixedly at the floor, "there's no doubt it would be much better for the children if they could stay together."

"Of course," said the young woman. "We never ought to have parted them."

Mr. Palfy was still looking hard at the floor. "We have a lot to make up for." He cleared his throat. "Well, I consent to your—to your taking both children back to Munich."

She put her hand to her heart.

"Perhaps," he went on, "you'll let them come and stay with me for a month every year?"

She did not answer, so he went on, "Or three weeks? Or at least two? I don't suppose you believe me, but I'm really very fond of both of them."

"Why shouldn't I believe you?" he heard her say.

He shrugged his shoulders. "I have not given much proof of it."

"Yes, you have—at Lottie's sickbed," she answered. "But how do you know that they'll be as happy as we want them to be, if they grow up without a father?"

"But they certainly couldn't grow up without you."

"Oh, Arnold! Don't you see what they really want, even though they don't dare say it?"

"Of course I do." He went to the window. "Of course I know what they want." He tugged impatiently at the window catch. "They want you and me to stay together."

"They want a father *and* a mother—our twins! Is that selfish of them?" asked the young woman eagerly.

"No, but wishes needn't be selfish to be unattainable." He stood by the window like a little boy who has been stood in the corner and defiantly refuses to come out again.

"Why is it unattainable?"

He turned in surprise. "You ask *me* that? After all that has happened?"

She looked at him earnestly and gave a scarcely perceptible nod. Then she said, "Yes. After all that has happened!"

Lisa was leaning against the door, one eye glued to the keyhole. Lottie was at her side, both hands stretched out, the fingers crossed.

"Oh, oh, oh!" cried Lisa. "Daddy's giving Mommy a kiss!"

Quite contrary to her usual custom, Lottie pushed her sister roughly aside and peered through the keyhole.

"Well?" asked Lisa. "Is he still doing it?"

"No," whispered Lottie, standing up with a radiant smile. "Now Mommy's giving Daddy a kiss."

Then the twins hooted with glee and fell into each other's arms.

Mr. Preiss is surprised · A principal tells a funny story ·
The front page of the Munich Illustrated *· A*
new name plate on an old door · Making up for
lost happiness · "And twins every time!"

Mr. Benno Preiss, the experienced old registrar of the first
district of Vienna, was performing a marriage which, in spite
of all his experience, caused him occasional twinges of mis-
giving. The bride was the divorced wife of the bridegroom.
The two terrifyingly similar ten-year-old girls were the daughters of the happy couple. One witness—an artist, Anton Gabel
by name—was not wearing a tie. And just to even things up,
the other witness—a certain Dr. Strobel—had brought a dog.
And the dog made such a commotion in the vestibule, where
it ought to have been left, that it had to be brought in and
allowed to take part in the ceremony. A dog as witness at a
wedding! Really, what were things coming to!

Lottie and Lisa sat reverently on their chairs and were as
happy as princesses. And they were not only happy but proud,
very proud indeed. For all this marvelous, unbelievable happiness was due to them. What would have happened to their

poor parents if it had not been for the children?

Well, then. And it had not been easy, either, to keep one's mouth shut and play the role of fate. Adventures, tears, anxiety, lies, despair, illness—nothing had been spared them. Not a thing!

After the ceremony Mr. Gabel whispered to Mr. Palfy, and the two men, each with artistic temperament, twinkled mysteriously at each other. But why they whispered and twinkled no one knew except themselves.

All that Mrs. Horn—formerly Palfy and now Palfy for the second time—had heard her ex- and present husband say was, "Too early?" Then he turned to her and went on fluently, "I've got an idea. Do you know what? We'll drive around to the school and register Lottie."

"Lottie! But Lottie's been there for—oh yes, of course. You're quite right."

Mr. Palfy gave Mrs. Palfy a tender look. "I should say so indeed."

Mr. Kilian, principal of the girls' school, was genuinely flabbergasted when Mr. Palfy and his wife registered a second daughter, who appeared to be completely identical with the first. But, as an old schoolteacher, he had had many experiences no less remarkable, and so he soon recovered his balance.

When the new pupil had been officially entered in the big register, he leaned back comfortably in his chair. "As a young assistant teacher," he said, "I once had an experience about which I should like to tell you. One Easter a new boy came to the school. He came from a poor home but he was as clean as could be and, as I soon found, a very good student. He made great progress. In arithmetic he was soon the best in the class. But he varied. For some time I was mystified. Then I thought, 'This is most extraordinary—sometimes he does the problems like a calculating machine without a single mistake. At other times he is much slower, and much less accurate.' "

The principal paused for effect, and his eyes twinkled benevolently at Lisa and Lottie. "At last I hit on the following plan: I noted down in a book the days when the boy did his arithmetic well and the days when he did it badly. And my plan produced a very strange result. On Mondays, Wednesdays, and Fridays he was good; on Tuesdays, Thursdays, and Saturdays he was bad."

"Think of that!" said Mr. Palfy. And the two little girls moved excitedly on their chairs.

"I went on making those notes for six weeks," continued the old gentleman. "It never altered. Mondays, Wednesdays, and Fridays, good. Tuesdays, Thursdays, and Saturdays, bad. So one fine day I went around to his parents' home and informed them of my puzzling observation. They looked at each other, half embarrassed, half amused, and then the husband said, 'I guess what you say is about right, sir.' Then he whistled, and two boys came running in from the next room. *Two*. The same height, the same looks in every respect. 'They're twins,' said the wife. 'Sepp is good at arithmetic and Toni is—the other.' When I recovered a little, I said, 'But tell me, why don't you send both boys to school?' And the father answered, 'We're poor, sir. The two boys have only one good suit be-between them.' "

The Palfys laughed. Mr. Kilian beamed, and Lisa cried, "That's an idea! We'll do the same!"

"You just dare!" said Mr. Kilian, threatening her with his finger. "Oh dear, no. Miss Gestettner and Miss Bruckbaur will have enough trouble without that!"

"Especially," said Lisa, carried away, "if we do our hair the same way and change places."

The principal clapped his hands above his head and gave other signs of being on the verge of desperation. "Terrible!" he cried. "And what will happen later on, when you are young ladies and someone wants to marry you?"

"Since we look the same," said Lottie thoughtfully, "we're sure to have the same man fall in love with us both."

"And we're sure both to fall in love with the same man," cried Lisa. "Then we shall both have to marry him. That's the best way. Mondays, Wednesdays, and Fridays I shall be his wife. And Tuesdays, Thursdays, and Saturdays it will be Lottie's turn."

"And if he doesn't happen to try you out at arithmetic," said Mr. Palfy laughing, "he'll never notice that he has two wives instead of one."

Mr. Kilian got up from his chair. "Poor fellow," he remarked pityingly.

Mrs. Palfy smiled. "But there'll be one good thing about it—
he'll have a day off on Sundays!"

As the newlywed—or, more precisely, the newly *re*-wed—
couple crossed the playground with the twins, morning recess
had just begun. Hundreds of little girls elbowed and were
elbowed in return, as they stared incredulously at Lisa and
Lottie.

At last Trudie succeeded in fighting her way through as
far as the twins. Panting for breath, she looked from one to
the other. Her first word was, "Well!" Then she turned with
an injured expression to Lisa. "First you make me promise not
to say a word about it at school, and then the two of you come
along as bold as brass!"

"It was I who made you promise," corrected Lottie.

"Now you can go ahead and tell everybody," said Lisa
graciously. "Tomorrow morning we're both coming."

Then Mr. Palfy forced his way through the crowd like an
icebreaker, and piloted his family to the school gates. Trudie
meanwhile became the victim of her schoolmates' curiosity.
They pushed her up to the branch of a rowan tree, where she
told everything she knew to the listening crowd of girls.

The bell rang. Recess was over. Or so you would have thought.

The teachers went back to the classrooms. The classrooms were empty. The teachers went to the windows and looked down with shocked expressions into the playground. The playground was packed. The teachers crowded into the principal's office to chorus their complaints.

"Sit down, ladies," he said. "My secretary has just brought me the current number of the *Munich Illustrated*. The front page is of great interest to this school. Would you mind reading it, Miss Bruckbaur?" He handed her the paper.

And now the teachers forgot—just like the girls in the playground—that recess was long since over.

Miss Irene Gerlach, smartly dressed as ever, was standing outside the Opera House, looking with astonishment at the front page of the *Munich Illustrated,* on which appeared a photograph of two little girls in braids. When she looked up her expression grew more astonished than ever. For a taxi had just paused at the crossing and in the taxi were two little girls with a gentleman who had once been well known to her and a lady whom she had hoped she would never know at all.

Lottie nudged her sister. "Look over there!"

"What? What is it?"

Lottie whispered, so softly that the words could scarcely be heard, "Miss Gerlach!"

"Where?"

"On the right. The one with a big hat and a paper in her hand." Lisa peered across at the smartly dressed lady. She would have liked to put out her tongue at her.

"What are you two up to?"

Goodness, now Mommy had probably noticed something!

But fortunately a distinguished old lady leaned out of a car that was waiting next to the taxi. She offered Mommy an illustrated paper, and said, smiling, "I think this might interest you."

Mrs. Palfy took the paper, looked at the front page, nodded and smiled, and passed it to her husband.

The cars began to move. The old lady nodded graciously.

The children climbed up on the seat beside Daddy, and inspected the photograph on the front page.

"That Mr. Appeldauer!" cried Lisa. "Fancy him letting us down like that!"

"And we thought we'd torn up *all* the prints," said Lottie.

"But he still had the negatives," explained Mommy, "so he could take hundreds of prints from them."

"What a good thing he did let you down," said Daddy. "If he hadn't, Mommy would never have discovered your secret, and then there would have been no wedding."

Lisa squirmed suddenly around and looked back at the Opera House. But far and wide there was no sign of Miss Gerlach.

Lottie said to her mother, "We'll write a letter of thanks to Mr. Appeldauer."

The "newlyweds" and the twins climbed the stairs of the house in Rotenturm Street.

Rosa in her Sunday best was waiting at the open door, grinning across the whole breadth of her face. She handed the bride a big bunch of flowers.

"Thank you very much, Rosa," returned Mrs. Palfy. "And I'm glad you've decided to stay with us."

Rosa nodded as vigorously and jerkily as a puppet in a Punch and Judy show. Then she stammered, "I ought to go back to the farm. To my father. But, you see, I'm so fond of Miss Lottie."

Conductor Palfy laughed. "That's not very polite to the other three of us, Rosa."

Not knowing what to say, Rosa shrugged her shoulders.

Mrs. Palfy came to the rescue. "Well, we can't stand at the door forever."

"Sorry, madam!" Rosa made way for them to pass.

"Just a second," said Mr. Palfy, with a broad grin. "I must just slip across to the other apartment."

The rest of the party froze. Surely he would not go back to his studio in Ring Street on his wedding day!

Mr. Palfy went to the door of Mr. Gabel's apartment, took out a key, and calmly unlocked it!

Lottie ran to him. On the door was a new name plate,

and on the new name plate was clearly engraved the one word, PALFY.

"Oh, Daddy!" she cried blissfully.

And then Lisa was at her side. She read the name plate, grabbed her sister by the collar, and began to execute a sort of victory dance. The old stairway shook at every joint.

"That's enough," cried Mr. Palfy at last. "Off you go to the kitchen and help Rosa." He looked at his watch. "I'm just going to show Mommy my studio, and in half an hour we'll have lunch. So when it's ready, just ring the bell." He took his young wife by the hand.

In the opposite doorway Lisa dropped a curtsy. "I hope we shall be good neighbors, Mr. Palfy."

Lisalottie Palfy took off her hat and coat. "What a surprise!" she said softly.

"A pleasant surprise?" he asked.

She nodded.

"It was Lottie's idea for some time before it was mine," he said slowly. "Gabel worked out every detail of the campaign and directed the battle of the moving vans."

"So this is why we had to call at the school?"

"Yes. Moving the grand piano gave the furniture wrestlers a little trouble!"

They went into his workroom. Resurrected from the drawer of his desk, the photograph of a young woman that dated from a past but unforgotten time stood on the piano. He put his arm around her. "On the third floor left, all four of us will be happy together, and on the third floor right, I shall be happy alone—but no further away than the other side of the wall."

"So much happiness!" She nestled against him.

"Anyhow, more than we deserve," he said seriously. "But not more than we can bear."

"I should never have believed it possible."

"What?"

"That one can make up for lost happiness, like a lesson one has missed at school."

He pointed to a picture on the wall. A small, earnest, childish face, as Gabel had drawn it, looked down from its frame at the two parents. "We owe every second of our new happiness," he said, "to our two children."

Lisa, decked in a kitchen apron, was standing on a chair, fastening to the wall with thumb tacks the front page of the *Munich Illustrated*.

"Beautiful!" said Rosa almost reverently.

Lottie, also in a kitchen apron, was bustling about at the stove.

Rosa dabbed a tear from the corner of her eye, sniffed gently, and asked, still standing in front of the picture, "Which of you two is really which?"

The two girls looked at each other, startled. Then they

looked at the picture pinned on the wall, and then at each other again.

"Well," began Lottie doubtfully.

"When Mr. Appeldauer took us, I think I was on the right," said Lisa, trying to remember.

Lottie shook her head slowly. "No, I was on the right . . . Or was I?"

The two girls craned their necks and stared at their portrait.

"Well, if you yourselves don't know which is which . . ." cried Rosa and began to laugh.

"No. We don't know ourselves!" shouted Lisa in delight. And then all three were laughing so loud that the noise penetrated to the studio next door.

And Mrs. Palfy asked, almost frightened, "Will you be able to work in a noise like that?"

He went to the piano and said, as he opened it, "Only in a noise like that!" And as the laughter next door died down, he played his wife the duet in E-flat major from the children's opera, and Rosa and the twins heard it and worked as quietly as mice so as not to miss a single note.

When the song was over Lottie asked shyly, "What's going to happen now, Rosa? Since Daddy and Mommy are both here with us again, do you think Lisa and I may have some brothers and sisters?"

"Of course," declared Rosa confidently. "Do you want them?"

"I should say we do," answered Lisa emphatically.

"Boys or girls?" asked Rosa.

"Boys *and* girls," said Lottie.

But Lisa cried from the bottom of her heart, "And twins every time!"

A CAST OF CHARACTERS TO DELIGHT THE HEARTS OF READERS!